"If I help Stacy, you're going to owe me big-time. You will cooperate with my plans for Nolie and Gabe's wedding." Claire was confident she knew what they wanted.

Brendan held out his hand for Claire to shake, his face serious but with a smile lurking in those changeable eyes. "Only if they agree. That's the other part of our deal."

"Fine. They'll agree."

"I told Stacy you'd be at the church tonight around nine." He got off her desk. "And we're having dinner with Nolie and Gabe at the Flanagan house at six. We can find out then what kind of wedding they *really* want."

She glared at him. "For a minister you're something of an opportunist, you know that?"

He grinned. "For a businesswoman, you're something of a do-gooder, Ms. Delaney. Maybe we bring out the best in each other."

"Or the worst."

He headed for the door. "I guess we'll find out, won't we?"

**Books by Marta Perry**

Love Inspired

## *MARTA PERRY*

has written everything from Sunday school curriculum to travel articles to magazine stories in twenty years of writing, but she feels she's found her home in the stories she writes for Love Inspired.

Marta lives in rural Pennsylvania, but she and her husband spend part of each year at their second home in South Carolina. When she's not writing, she's probably visiting her children and her beautiful grandchildren, traveling, or relaxing with a good book.

Marta loves hearing from readers and she'll write back with a signed bookplate or bookmark. Write to her c/o Steeple Hill Books, 233 Broadway, Suite 1001 New York, NY 10279, e-mail her at marta@martaperry.com, or visit her on the Web at www.martaperry.com.

# UNLIKELY HERO

## MARTA PERRY

Steeple
Hill®

Published by Steeple Hill Books™

STEEPLE HILL BOOKS

Steeple
Hill®

ISBN 0-373-87297-6

UNLIKELY HERO

Copyright © 2005 by Martha Johnson

This edition published by arrangement with Steeple Hill Books.

® and TM are trademarks of Steeple Hill Books, used under license. Trademarks indicated with ® are registered in the United States Patent and Trademark Office, the Canadian Trade Marks Office and in other countries.

www.SteepleHill.com

**Printed in U.S.A.**

Trust in the Lord with all your heart; do not depend
on your own understanding. Seek His will in
all you do and He will direct your paths.
—*Proverbs* 3:5–6

This story is dedicated to Alice Dyne, with love
and thanks for all she does for others.
And, as always, to Brian.

# Chapter One

"You're wrong, that's all." Claire Delany had a fleeting doubt about speaking that way to a minister, but dismissed it. No clerical collar would deter her from saying what she thought.

Not that Brendan Flanagan was wearing a clerical collar. She glanced at him as he held the door and then followed her from the church gym into a hallway that had classrooms on either side. Gray sweatpants and a navy sweatshirt, battered sneakers, disheveled chestnut brown hair tumbling onto his forehead. Only a hint of gravity in his lean face and hazel eyes suggested that he had anything more serious than a game of basketball on his mind.

"Maybe I am wrong." Brendan's voice, a baritone rumble, was mild. "But when Gabe asked me to officiate, I understood him to say they wanted a small, quiet wedding with no fuss."

"Gabe may have said that—" she tried the no-non-sense voice she was known for at work "—but I know what kind of wedding Nolie has dreamed of all her life. I don't want her to give up her dream wedding just because they're so busy right now with the new project."

The grant her best friend had recently received would let Nolie and Gabe expand their service animal project to many more disabled people. She understood how important that was, but Nolie shouldn't have to sacrifice having a memorable wedding because of it.

Brendan came to a halt next to a bulletin board covered with orange and yellow construction paper leaves, printed with what she supposed were children's names. She stopped, too, swinging to face him. He was tall, like all the Flanagan men, and even the two-inch heels she wore for work didn't give her enough height to confront him.

He was probably good at intimidating with his height, those keen eyes and that air of authority that went along with being a minister, but she wasn't going to let him force his views onto her, no matter how self-assured he was.

"Nolie is my closest friend," she said firmly. "If she doesn't have the time right now to handle the wedding arrangements, then I'll be happy to take care of them for her."

Brendan raised an eyebrow. "Gabe is my cousin as well as my friend and parishioner. And I intend to listen to what he says they want."

He had her on the parishioner business. Gabe was a member of Brendan's church. Nolie probably would be soon, as well. Her friend was being absorbed into the big, noisy Flanagan clan at a rapid rate, and Brendan's church was obviously an important part of their lives.

As for her—well, her mother had taken her to church when she was a child, but after her mother's death, her father hadn't set foot inside a church with her. Other than attending a wedding or two, she'd followed his pattern. Religion was a foreign country to her, one she didn't have any interest in exploring.

She tried another tack. "Maybe Gabe just doesn't care. A wedding is more for the bride, anyway."

Brendan's eyes weren't the Irish blue of his Flanagan cousins. Instead they were a mutable hazel, and at the moment they looked as remote, green and frosty as an Alpine lake.

"A wedding is a solemn event in the spiritual lives of two people, not an excuse for a party."

Now he really was putting on his minister hat. She was tempted to point out that the wedding decisions weren't really up to him, but he'd simply turn that argument back on her. They weren't up to her, either, until Gabe and Nolie agreed with her suggestions.

She'd already seen how close all the Flanagans were. The only way to win this was to have Pastor Brendan on her side. Then she could present Nolie with a fait accompli instead of a what-if.

"I'm not talking about turning the wedding into a riot, Pastor. Just making it beautiful and memorable. Surely you don't have any theological objections to that."

The sudden flash of humor in his eyes startled her. "Not theological, no. But we might not agree on what beautiful and memorable is."

"We won't know unless we try, will we?"

He studied her face for a long moment, as if wondering what lay beneath the surface. His steady gaze began to make her uneasy. She didn't have a smudge of mascara on her nose, did she?

"Fair enough," he said finally. "Let's take a look at the sanctuary and talk about what you have in mind."

His tone made it clear he was reserving judgment on her view of the wedding. That didn't matter. She'd swing him around to her way of thinking.

Brendan led the way back up the flight of stairs she'd come down. When she hadn't found him waiting in his office for their appointment, she'd followed the sound of thuds, bumps, and jeers to the gym, where he'd been playing basketball with a scruffy-looking bunch of teenagers.

Strange as it seemed, she'd apparently have to negotiate with the minister to get what she wanted. No, what *Nolie* would want. Failure wasn't part of her vocabulary. She and Nolie had a kinship that went deeper than friendship or sisterhood, and she'd give Nolie the wedding of her dreams even if she had to go through Brendan Flanagan to do it.

But she'd try a milder tactic first. She'd always found it useful in business to establish some sort of mutual ground. She glanced at him as they walked through another long hallway, this one lined with stained-glass windows. The brighter light picked out the fine lines fanning out from the corners of his eyes, suggesting that he took his responsibilities seriously.

"Was that some kind of a youth group you were working out with in the gym?"

He looked startled, as if he'd forgotten about those kids. "No, not exactly." He hesitated before going on. "This neighborhood has changed since Grace Church was built a hundred years ago. A lot of kids in the area don't have a church to call their own, or any place to hang out except the street corners."

"I've seen them." She frowned. "Frankly, most of the kids I've noticed hanging around the street corners aren't ones I'd care to invite into my church, if I had one."

"Reaching out to people who need help is the church's business." His look was faintly disapproving.

Claire stiffened. Whether he was a minister or not, he didn't have the right to disapprove just because she'd voiced her opinion.

Be agreeable, a little voice cautioned in her mind. You want to gain his cooperation, not put his back up.

"I guess Suffolk isn't just an old-fashioned market town anymore," she said.

He nodded, as if Claire were a pupil who'd gotten an answer right. "That's the problem exactly. People still think this is the kind of place where everyone has the same values, but it's not. Suffolk has become a mid-size city with a few city problems no one has figured out how to deal with yet."

"And you're the man to deal with them." She tried to keep the skepticism out of her voice.

"I'm trying. With God's help."

That was the sort of thing a politician might say, except that in Brendan's deep voice, it sounded genuine. If he insisted on bringing God into the discussion, she was definitely out of her depth. A Sunday school class when she was seven or eight hadn't prepared her for a debate on religious issues with a minister.

Well, that wasn't why she'd come here, in any event. She wanted his cooperation with the wedding. Aside from that, she didn't care how many juvenile delinquents Brendan let take advantage of him.

He opened a paneled oak door at the end of the hallway. They stepped into a vast, echoing space, dimly lit by a bank of recessed lights at the front.

"This is the sanctuary. By the way, I draw the line at live doves let loose in here."

The glimmer of humor he showed again reassured her. Maybe he wouldn't be too difficult to deal with. "Not even one or two?"

"Not even." He fumbled along the wall for a light switch, and the overhead chandeliers came on with a blaze of light, making the sanctuary spring to life. "As you can see, there's a center aisle. I'm told wedding planners like that."

Claire looked the length of the sanctuary. The cream walls were accentuated with walnut arches and wainscoting, and a burgundy carpet crossed the front and swept up the aisles.

"It's perfect." She could visualize Nolie coming down that center aisle, past pews decorated with flowers and ribbons. She could almost hear the murmurs of appreciation.

No, that wasn't a murmur. It was a stifled sob.

Brendan seemed to hear the sound at the same time she did. He spun toward a pew half-hidden by one of the columns. What she'd taken for a coat thrown over it was actually a woman, huddled into herself on the cushioned seat.

No, not a woman. This was barely more than a girl, wearing threadbare jeans and a tattered T-shirt. Her long dark hair hung down to screen her face.

Claire took a step forward, and then stopped. This wasn't any of her business.

"Stacy?" Brendan knelt next to the kid, his hand gripping the pew's carved arm. His voice was soft with concern. "What's wrong?"

Obviously he knew the girl, and he'd shifted into minister mode. All his attention was concentrated on her, as if he'd forgotten Claire was there.

That was undoubtedly her cue to back away. Even though she didn't want to put it off, their wedding consultation would have to wait until another time.

"I should leave," she said.

The girl looked up at the sound of her voice, her hair falling back from a too-thin face. Claire's heart seemed to stop and then resume beating in slow, threatening thuds. The kid's cheek was puffed out, and one eye had been blackened.

It wasn't just the obvious signs of abuse that turned her stomach and made her want to flee. It was the look in the girl's eyes—frightened and accepting all at once, like a dumb animal that couldn't escape.

She knew the look. It was the one she used to see in her mirror.

Brendan put his hand gently on Stacy's and fought down the tidal wave of black anger that threatened to overwhelm him. He couldn't give in to the anger. That would make him no better than the person who'd done this. He had to concentrate on her.

"What happened, Stacy? Did Ted do this to you?"

Stacy's boyfriend was the likely culprit. The girl's mother seemed to play little role in Stacy's life, as far as he'd been able to find out the few times Stacy had stopped by the church with some of the neighborhood teens.

"No!" Her response was emphatic, and her hand flew up to shield her eye. "Ted wouldn't hurt me. He loves me." She jerked away from him, as if ready to flee.

"Right. I'll bet you walked into a door."

Claire's voice startled him. In his concern for Stacy, he'd forgotten she was there.

He frowned at her. Sarcasm wasn't what Stacy needed at a time like this.

Claire was looking at the girl, and something in her

gaze gave him pause. She looked—he couldn't put his finger on it, but it was almost as if she saw something familiar in Stacy.

He gave himself a mental shake. Claire was all chilly edges and expensive sophistication, from the top of her shining mahogany hair to the tips of the shoes that had probably cost more than he'd made last month. She couldn't have anything in common with one of his lost street kids.

"Yeah, that's right. A door." Stacy snapped the words at Claire, but she leaned back against the pew, her impulse to run apparently vanishing. "I was clumsy."

Something unspoken seemed to pass between her and Claire.

"Easy to do in the dark," Claire agreed. She leaned over, touching Stacy's chin to tilt her head back for a better look. "You ought to get some ice on that shiner."

Her voice was matter-of-fact, almost cool, but Stacy appeared to respond to it. She nodded. "Yeah. Guess so."

Brendan sat back on his heels. Nothing in his brief acquaintance with Claire Delany had led him to believe she could relate to anyone outside her yuppie world, but he couldn't deny the evidence of his own eyes.

"We can get some ice in the kitchen," he said. "But it seems to me you need a place to stay tonight. Someplace where you won't be walking into any more doors."

Stacy shrugged. "I'll be okay. I could just sleep here." She patted the cushioned pew.

He could imagine the reaction of some of his parishioners if they learned he'd let a kid spend the night in the sanctuary. He'd already heard some sharp comments about letting neighborhood teens use the gym.

"I don't think that's a good idea," he said gently. "There's a shelter—"

"No!" Stacy shot upright, clutching her jacket with both hands. "I'm not going to any shelter. I can take care of myself."

That was just what she couldn't do, but she'd never admit it.

"Look, Stacy, you need a safe place."

"No shelter." Her mouth set in a stubborn line, and she grabbed the back of the pew. "I better get going."

"Wait." He put his hand on his arm. He couldn't let her walk away. "Just give me a minute, okay? I need to talk to Claire about something."

She gave him a wary look, but something in his expression must have allayed her suspicion. She nodded, subsiding back onto the seat.

He straightened, taking Claire's arm to draw her back to the doorway. "I'm sorry about this." He lowered his voice. "I'm afraid we'll have to postpone our conversation."

That determined jaw of Claire's seemed to get a little firmer. "I suppose so. What are you going to do with the girl?"

He kept his voice soft. No need for Stacy to hear. "Find a safe place for her to stay tonight. One of my parishioners will take her in, I'm sure."

"And what about after that? A bed for the night doesn't solve the problem." Something he couldn't interpret shadowed the deep brown of Claire's eyes.

"It gives us time. By tomorrow she'll be ready to talk with me." He hoped.

Claire's face tightened. "By tomorrow she'll run right back to the person who gave her that shiner."

"That's a pretty cynical assessment."

"It's a practical one."

There was some undercurrent in her words that he didn't quite get. "Anyway, I'm sorry about this." He touched her hand lightly in mute apology.

Claire looked up at his touch, something startled and wary in her gaze, and then she took a step back. She glanced past him to where Stacy slumped in the pew.

"Take care of yourself, Stacy."

She smiled at the girl. His breath caught. That smile transformed Claire's sharp face for a moment, turning her into someone lively and caring.

"Thanks for understanding," he said, shaking himself out of it.

She nodded and pushed open the door behind her. "I'll check in with you tomorrow morning. I have to get going on the wedding. We only have a month."

Caution stirred. "We'd better talk with Gabe and Nolie before making any decisions." We? How had he gotten into this, anyway?

"Of course." Her smile suggested that she was taking his cooperation for granted. "We'll do that."

The door swung shut behind her, and he tried to dismiss an uneasy feeling. He'd managed nervous grooms, tearful brides and overbearing mothers in his time. He could surely handle one determined best friend.

In the meantime, he had Stacy to take care of. He'd better find a parishioner to take her for the night. Then he could—

Well, then he could try to find Ted. The black anger roiled again, under control but always there, always warning him of what he could become if he weren't careful.

*Please, Lord.* He didn't need to form the rest of the prayer. God had heard it often enough from him.

Stacy wasn't the only one who should probably wait until tomorrow to discuss this.

"Come on, Stacy. Let's get that ice for your face while I make a few calls."

He had to focus on Stacy's needs right now. Even as he told himself that, Claire's unexpected smile blossomed again in his memory, softening the jagged edges of her personality and turning her into someone he wanted to know better.

Maybe, if it meant seeing that smile more often, working with Claire on the wedding wouldn't be such a bad idea after all.

Claire swatted at the insistent alarm clock with a groan. She hadn't gotten her usual eight hours, thanks to Pastor Brendan and that girl. Stacy's battered face had refused to be dismissed from her mind. Even after she'd fallen asleep, the image had intruded on her dreams.

She pushed herself out of bed, toes curling into the plush carpet, and padded across to the bathroom. Those bad dreams hadn't haunted her in a number of years, until last night. Her reaction to the girl had proved they weren't banished entirely.

Fortunately, she didn't have to be involved in the situation any further. Helping people like Stacy was Brendan's business, not hers.

The only problem was that she could understand something Brendan never would about how that girl was feeling right now. He thought a safe place for the night and a good talk would change Stacy's life.

He was wrong. She could tell Brendan that, but she didn't intend to. No one in Suffolk knew about her past except Nolie, and that was the way she wanted it.

She showered and dressed for the day with quick efficiency, her morning routine down to an exact science. She'd never been late in all the years she'd been Harvey Gray's assistant. She wouldn't give her boss a chance to think he could get along without her.

She went down the steps, running her hand along the smoothly polished railing. The extra little touches of finely turned woodwork and custom fittings had sold her on the town house, and she hadn't regretted that decision for a moment. A rising young executive needed a proper setting, and each time she made a mortgage payment, she reflected on the value accruing.

She glanced at her watch. She was early, and Brendan's church was on her way. She may as well stop and see when they could meet again about the wedding. She could make a fresh start at persuading him she knew what she was doing.

The ten minutes it took to drive to the church was just long enough to make her wonder if that was really why she was going in person instead of calling. It wasn't because she wanted to know what had happened to Stacy. And it certainly wasn't because she wanted to see Brendan Flanagan again.

She parked at the curb and walked briskly to the office wing. She'd be quick and businesslike. That was the way to deal with him.

No one was in the outer office. Apparently Brendan's secretary didn't come in this early. She knocked on the door to his study and it swung open. Brendan sat tipped back in his chair as if he'd been there all night. He righted the chair at the sight of her, running one hand through disheveled hair that was the same glossy brown as the horse chestnuts children collected from beneath the tree in the town square in the fall.

"Claire. What brings you here so early?"

"Did you spend the night here?" She probably shouldn't ask such a personal question. They weren't friends. It wasn't her business where he spent his nights.

He got up, stretching, the movement making her aware of the long, lean strength of him. "Only part of it."

No, Brendan Flanagan was definitely not her image

of a minister. His worn jeans and navy sweater, combined with that certain tough something about his jaw, made him look more like a firefighter, like the rest of his family.

"Ministers keep odd hours, then. Maybe you should have gone into the family business instead."

"Firefighting? Some days I think it might be easier." He shrugged. "That's in my blood, anyway. I'm the fire department chaplain."

"I didn't realize." Although she wasn't surprised, now that she thought about it. All the Flanagans were involved in firefighting, and it seemed to be a source of family pride.

"Won't you sit down?" Brendan gestured toward the black vinyl armchair that sat in front of his gray metal desk. His congregation certainly hadn't put much money into furnishing the minister's office. The wall of books behind him was undoubtedly the most expensive thing here.

"I'm on my way to work." She reminded herself of why she'd come. "Let's just set another time to get together about the wedding."

"Sure thing." He flipped open a desk calendar and slid on a pair of black-rimmed glasses to consult it. "But I still want to talk with Gabe and Nolie about this first."

Obviously he didn't intend to take her word for what Nolie wanted. "Fine." She bit off the word. "I'll give Nolie a call after I get to the office. Maybe we can get this cleared up today, so I can get going on things."

She turned, then hesitated and reversed. It wouldn't hurt to ask. "How's Stacy? Did you find a place for her last night?"

"Yes. She stayed at my aunt and uncle's house."

She might have known. The Flanagan clan seemed to stick together on everything. "Have you had that talk with her yet?"

"Not exactly." Something wary and cautious shadowed his eyes, making them look more gray than green.

She could interpret that look. "Something went wrong. What?"

"Nothing. Well, not exactly." He so clearly didn't want to tell her that it was almost funny. "Aunt Siobhan called. When they got up this morning, Stacy was gone. So was fifty dollars from my uncle's wallet."

She'd been that desperate once. The memory of it made her stomach churn. She forced the feeling away, angry at Brendan for making her remember. "I hate to say I told you so, but—"

He frowned. "Look, sometimes these kids have to test the boundaries. She's trying to figure out if we're people she can count on. She'll come back."

"I hope you're right about that, Pastor."

But she didn't think he was. In Stacy's position, she probably would have used the money to run. Or maybe she'd have gone right back into the bad situation. That had happened more often than she wanted to recall.

"But you think I'm wrong." He studied her face intently, as if he'd looked beneath the skin to her inner heart. "Why are you so sure?"

The sick feeling was back. Being around Brendan brought out all kinds of strong feelings, and she didn't want any of them.

"That's just another situation where you and I don't agree, I'm afraid." She pushed the subject away. "I'd better get going."

"Wait a second." He held out one hand, smiling at her. "I'll make a deal with you."

She frowned, searching for immunity to the masculine wallop that easy smile contained. The Flanagan men seemed to have more than their fair share of male magnetism.

"What kind of a deal?"

"We both think we know what Gabe and Nolie want. If you're right about Nolie really wanting a big wedding, I'll help you pull it off."

She looked at that. She didn't see a catch. "A deal has to have two sides. What's the other one?"

"If I'm right about Stacy, then you'll give me a hand with my teens."

She stared at him blankly. "*Your* teens?"

"The kids you saw last night." Sudden enthusiasm made his eyes sparkle. "I'm trying to help some of them learn to apply for jobs. You're an expert at the business world. Seems as if you were made for the project."

"Oh, no." Words couldn't express how little she

wanted to do that. "I'm not a do-gooder. Besides, I'll be too busy with the wedding."

"Not if you're right. If you're right, I'll be helping you with the wedding."

She *was* right. So what did she have to lose?

"What do you say?" His eyebrows lifted in a challenge. "Do we have a deal?"

"All right. We have a deal."

"Fine." He held out his hand, as if to seal the bargain. She took it, and his fingers closed on hers, generating a wave of warmth that dumbfounded her. For an instant Brendan looked startled, as if that warmth had hit him, too.

She pulled her hand free and looked at her watch. "I have to go. I'm going to be late for work." That was something else to chalk up against him.

The less she saw of Pastor Brendan, the better. He had a way of upsetting her equilibrium, and she didn't like things getting out of her control.

So why had she just made a deal to work with him on the wedding arrangements? And with his group of juvenile delinquents, too?

Well, that part of it wasn't going to happen. Unfortunately, she knew she was right about Stacy.

As for Brendan— She took a deep breath. Whatever effect the man had on her, she'd just have to ignore it until it went away.

## Chapter Two

Claire frowned at her computer screen. The report she was compiling seemed to have lost its charm. The dry recital of statistics and probabilities faded into a background for Stacy's troubled face.

Or maybe for Brendan's, looking at her with that quizzical smile of his.

She swung away from the screen, exasperated. It was bad enough that Brendan had made her late for work for the first time in—well, ever. It was worse that he kept intruding on her concentration now that she was here. Work was too important to let anything else interfere with it.

No woman had ever risen to the level of assistant to the president of Gray Enterprises, until she'd managed it. She wasn't about to stop there, either. *CEO*. That had a nice sound to it. Harvey Gray wouldn't want to stay active in the company he'd founded forever. There was no reason why his trusted right hand shouldn't become his successor, if she played her cards right. Then she'd be safe.

Safe? She rethought her choice of words, appalled. Safety had nothing to do with it. She would never let herself be a victim again, regardless of her position. It was just that encounter with Stacy that upset her.

She glanced around her office, with its Berber carpeting and built-in walnut shelves. When she moved up the ladder, she'd have mahogany, and the door with the frosted-glass window would be replaced by a solid one.

Those little nuances spelled out one's relative importance to the company. She didn't have to be content with a cubicle any longer, and if the frosted glass served to isolate her from colleagues, that was just part of success.

A tap at the door startled her. She frowned at the shadow behind the frosted glass before taking a quick look into her pocket mirror. It was probably just her secretary, but it wouldn't do to be caught looking less than her best.

"Come in."

But it wasn't her secretary. Brendan Flanagan, his clerical collar looking decidedly out of place in the capitalist confines of Gray Enterprises, popped his head around the door.

"Hope I'm not disturbing you."

He was, but she could hardly say so. "How did you find me?" Actually, that was silly. He could have asked Nolie, if he wanted to know anything about her.

He let the door swing shut and crossed to the desk. "I knew you worked for Harvey Gray. Harvey is one of my parishioners."

So maybe he wasn't as out of place here as she'd assumed.

"I didn't realize." She gestured to the visitor's chair, which was placed at a distance from her desk—a careful calculation to preserve her air of authority. "Sit down."

Instead of taking the seat she'd indicated, Brendan propped himself against her desk, intruding into her space. She edged her chair back an inch.

"What brings you here?"

And why was she letting his presence make her feel uncomfortable in her own office? She glanced around the room, mentally contrasting its elegance with the Spartan surroundings of Brendan's office. This room never failed to assure her that she had it made.

He pulled something out of his suit pocket and put it on her pristine blotter. A fifty-dollar bill.

She stared at it, uncomprehending. "What's that?"

"It's from Stacy."

"Stacy." That brought her gaze to search his face. "She's turned up?" She hadn't realized until that moment that she'd actually been worrying about that ungrateful kid.

Brendan leaned toward her across the desk, his smile inviting her to join him in celebrating. "An hour ago she walked into the church, apologizing. I told her she owed my aunt and uncle the apology, not me."

"All of you, I think." She was more relieved than she'd have thought possible. After all, she barely knew the girl, and that was the way she planned to keep it. "I guess that means she's going to let you help her."

He lifted an eyebrow, as if she should know the answer to that. "Not exactly."

"What do you mean, not exactly?" A sense of foreboding gripped her.

"Stacy wants to talk. I figure she can be your first project."

She could only stare at him, appalled at the very idea. "Project? What on earth are you talking about?"

He waved the bill again. "Our deal. Remember? You agreed that if I was right to trust Stacy, you'd help out with my teens."

She couldn't have agreed to any such thing, could she? "I didn't."

"You did." His lips twitched. "You're not by any chance trying to get out of our deal, are you, Ms. Delany?"

Of course she was. Her mind scrambled frantically for an excuse he'd accept. "You asked me to help them prepare for jobs, that's all."

Not deal with abuse. Her stomach clenched.

"If Stacy thought she could get along all right on her own, she'd be less likely to stay in a bad relationship."

He was more right about that than he probably knew, but that didn't mean she could do this.

"Stacy wouldn't want to talk to me. I wasn't even nice to her."

"Oddly enough, that seems to have made an impression on her. She said you were real." He shrugged. "As opposed to me, apparently."

"Does that bother you?" She jumped at the chance to turn the subject toward him, but he just shook his head.

"This isn't about me. It's about Stacy. And the agreement you made." He leaned toward her across the desk again, his eyes so intent they seemed to probe her soul.

She drew back, putting a few more inches between herself and that magnetic gaze. "I'm not a social worker. I can't help her."

"You don't know that. For some reason, Stacy seems to relate to you."

Because the girl sensed that Claire had once been where she was? Nonsense. She couldn't possibly.

"That's very flattering, but I've got my hands full already with my work and the wedding. I can't take on anything else."

"You said you would."

She opened her mouth to protest, but he had her, and they both knew it.

There was still a way out of this. If she told Brendan about her past, he'd trip all over himself apologizing for trying to involve her in something so painful to a person with her history.

She wouldn't. She wouldn't give him a reason to look at her with pity. Nobody got to pity her.

She came to a reluctant conclusion. "I just have to talk to her, right?"

He shrugged. "I think your conscience will tell you what to do from there."

If he only knew. "I wouldn't be so sure of that, Pastor. My conscience is pretty elastic after a number of years in the business world."

"I trust you."

Really, that smile of his ought to be outlawed.

"If I do this, you're going to owe me big-time."

"What do you want?"

"We both know that. You cooperate with my plans for the wedding."

"Only if Nolie and Gabe agree. That's the other part of our deal, remember?"

"Fine. They'll agree." She was confident she knew what Nolie wanted, and Gabe was so in love that he'd do anything that made Nolie happy.

"Then I guess you have a deal, Ms. Delany." Brendan held out his hand, his face serious but with a smile lurking in those changeable eyes.

She put her hand in his, her apprehension stirring. That wave of warmth hit again. Being prepared didn't seem to prevent it.

She had to catch her breath before she could speak evenly. "All right, a deal. When do you want me to get together with Stacy?"

"I told her you'd be at the church tonight around nine. Usually some of the kids stop by then, and that'll make her feel safer." He got off her desk. "And we're having dinner with Gabe and Nolie at the Flanagan house at six. We can find out then what kind of wedding they want."

She glared at him. "You were taking an awful lot for granted, weren't you?"

"We both get what we want. What's wrong with that?" He gave her an innocent look she didn't buy.

"For a minister you're something of an opportunist, you know that?"

He grinned. "For a businesswoman, you're something of a do-gooder, Ms. Delany. Maybe we bring out the best in each other."

"Or the worst."

He headed for the door. "I guess we'll find out, won't we?"

Brendan had been trying to figure out Claire's opinion of the Flanagan family throughout the whole meal, and he didn't quite have it pegged yet. He forked a bite of his Aunt Siobhan's excellent apple crumb pie into his mouth and watched while Claire parried Uncle Joe's questions about the inner workings of Gray Enterprises.

Claire's polish and sophistication would probably make her at home anywhere, but she definitely hadn't wanted to attend this family dinner. She'd come, because he hadn't given her much choice if she wanted his co-operation with the wedding, but she seemed to be doing a great job of resisting the famous Flanagan charm.

He glanced around the long oval table that had been

the scene of countless family dinners over three generations of Flanagans. The crowd was smaller than usual tonight, out of deference to the fact that Gabe and Nolie were supposed to be having a quiet evening to plan their wedding.

Only Seth, the brother who came next after Gabe, sat at the table, coaxing his toddler son to try a bite of apple. Davy grinned, snatched the apple slice, and rubbed it through his fine, red-gold hair.

This had been home to Brendan for so long that he sometimes managed to forget his earlier life. Sometimes, but not for long. His father had been Uncle Joe's brother, after all, and an innocent phrase or gesture could bring that past surging back.

Joe held center stage at the moment, as he so often did, while Siobhan watched him, quietly smiling. He'd turn soon to his favorite subject.

"And did you know that all the Flanagans were members of the Suffolk Fire Department, Ms. Delany?"

"I've heard something about that, yes." Claire's gaze met Brendan's. "I guess Brendan broke the family tradition, didn't he?"

"You'd think that, but you'd be wrong," Joe said triumphantly. "Brendan might be a minister, but he's also the chaplain of the fire department."

Claire's eyebrows lifted. "Yes, he told me. He's talented, isn't he?"

"That's our Brendan. And he doesn't just go through the motions. He's a fully qualified firefighter, too. I'd

count on him to take the hose in just as much as I would
Gabe or Seth or Ryan."

"Leave me out of it," Gabe said. He smiled at Nolie,
and the love that shone between them was so bright it
hurt to look. "I've got another full-time job now."

"And a good one it is, too," Joe said quickly.

After an accident on the job left Gabe prone to sei-
zures that ended his career, they'd all feared he'd never
be himself again. Then Nolie and the service animals
she trained had given him a new purpose in life.

Max, Gabe's seizure alert dog, lay beside his chair.
Gabe and Nolie were totally involved in expanding her
services to give more people a fresh start.

They all owed a great deal to Nolie. Brendan wondered, not for the first time, at the strong bond between
Nolie and Claire. They seemed such total opposites.
Nolie was all warmth and caring, more comfortable in
jeans working with her animals than anywhere else.

Claire didn't look as if she ever wore anything as casual as jeans. Even the clothes she'd chosen for a simple
family dinner, black slacks and cream silk shirt, de-
clared that. Against the shirt, her hair was a helmet of
burnished copper.

He'd have guessed Claire was the type of woman to
have few women friends, obsessed as she seemed to be
with her career. Whatever the secret to her bond with
Nolie was, Gabe probably knew it, but Gabe wasn't
telling.

"Let's take our coffee into the living room and be

comfortable," Siobhan suggested. "We can talk about the wedding there."

Brendan slid his arm around his aunt's waist as they got up. "That was a wonderful meal." He kissed her cheek. "As always."

"You should know," Seth gibed. "You're always here."

"I'm invited," he retorted. "What's your excuse?"

Since young Davy chose that moment to throw a bit of apple at his father, Seth didn't respond. Brendan escaped to the living room.

Seth would get his revenge at some point, of course. That was part of being more like brothers than cousins.

Joe was giving Claire the grand tour of the wall that was covered with fire department photos and citations. He glanced at Gabe, who rolled his eyes. There was no sidetracking Uncle Joe when he got started on his favorite topic.

"That picture is me and my two brothers when we joined up, more years ago than I care to remember," Joe said, gesturing to a faded black-and-white photo. "We thought we were pretty hot stuff the first time we put those uniforms on."

Claire leaned closer, studying the picture as if she really were interested in Flanagan family history. "Which one is Brendan's father?"

His stomach clenched, but at least she'd asked Joe, not him. Joe pointed.

"That's my brother John, Brendan's dad. He was a year younger than me."

And a million miles different in temperament. But probably his uncle was able to remember some of the good things about his little brother.

Claire took a step or two along the wall, looking at one citation after another. Nobody could fault the Flanagans when it came to courage. They had more than their share of citations attesting to that.

"Distinguished Fire Service Award," Claire read. "John Patrick Flanagan." She glanced at him. "This was your father's."

He nodded. "The highest award given by the department." He was pleased that his voice sounded so level.

"I should think you'd want to have this in your office," she said. "Or your home."

How he kept his expression steady he wasn't sure. What was it with this woman? How could she manage to put her finger right on the sore spot and push?

"Aunt Siobhan keeps the awards," he said lightly. "I wouldn't want to leave a hole in her display."

He carried his coffee to a chair and sat, only to discover that Gabe was watching him with concern. Okay, maybe he wasn't hiding his feelings as well as he thought, at least not from Gabe, who knew him better than anyone. But Claire would never guess.

He glanced at his watch. "I'm sorry to interrupt the grand tour, Uncle Joe, but maybe we'd better get started on the wedding arrangements. I have to be back at the church by nine."

Uncle Joe nodded, but Gabe gave him a quizzical

look. "I thought we'd already decided. A simple, quiet ceremony, just family and a few friends. Nolie and I are too busy with the expansion project to do anything else."

Some of his tension eased. Surely Claire would see that they had to do this Gabe and Nolie's way.

"Claire has some other ideas—" he began, but Claire interrupted him.

"I'm the closest thing Nolie has to family." Her voice was determined. "I want to give her a real wedding with all the trimmings. She's only going to do this once. It should be a day to remember."

He waited for Nolie to insist that what she wanted was the simple ceremony Gabe had talked about.

"Claire, I can't let you do that," Nolie said, her blue eyes troubled. "It's too expensive, and besides, we just don't have enough time. We're so busy with the farm we can't take care of all those arrangements."

"That's why I want you to let me do it." The firm set of Claire's jaw suggested that neither money nor time would deter her. "You should have a perfect wedding." Her look softened. "You and Gabe deserve it. Let me do this for you—it would be my gift to you both. Please."

Gabe looked horrified for just one instant. Then he looked at Nolie and obviously saw what they all saw— that moment of sheer longing before she closed the door on the idea and shook her head.

"I agree," Siobhan said unexpectedly. "So there's not much time. So what? Goodness knows we've put on plenty of parties on a moment's notice in the past. A wedding's far more important."

If Aunt Siobhan had gone over to the enemy, they were really in trouble.

"The ceremony is the important thing," Brendan said, but he had the sinking feeling no one was listening to him.

Siobhan, Claire and Nolie were suddenly all talking at once, and words like "shower," "flowers" and "lace" floated to the surface like spray tossed up by a wave.

He met Gabe's gaze. Gabe gave a rueful grin. "Forget it, Bren," he said. "We've been outvoted. I guess it's going to be a wedding with a capital W."

"I guess so."

Claire cast him a triumphant look, as if she'd heard his capitulation over the babble of voices.

It appeared he'd be spending a great deal of time with Claire over the next month. That idea seemed to be making him feel ridiculously cheerful.

Claire walked slowly from the church parlor, where she and Stacy had been talking, toward Brendan's study. She shouldn't feel so at home in the church after only a few days. After all, she hadn't been in a church before that for twenty-some years.

Nevertheless, here she was going in search of the pastor, just like any one of his faithful parishioners. Brendan would probably be as horrified at that thought as she was.

But she wasn't really looking for his advice, was

she? After all, she knew more about what Stacy was going through than he ever could. Still, she felt compelled to check in with him.

The study door was propped open, and as soon as he saw her, Brendan came toward her, hand outstretched in welcome. "How did it go? Is there anything I can do?"

She didn't want to admit the pleasure she felt at the sight of him. "At least she's given up the attacking door story and admitted Ted hit her."

"That's good." He studied her face. "You look all in. Takes something out of you, doesn't it?"

She nodded. He couldn't know just how much. "I don't know how you manage to do this all the time. Of course, I suppose your regular congregation doesn't present problems like this very often."

He gave a short bark of laughter. "You don't know much about congregations if you think that." He gestured her toward a chair and opened the small refrigerator under a microwave on the opposite wall. "A cold soda?"

"Sounds good." She watched as he popped the lids on two soda cans. Some tall men were awkward, but she'd already noticed that Brendan went about the simplest tasks with an easy economy of movement. He carried the soda to her, then folded himself into the chair opposite her, rather than going back to his seat behind the desk.

"So every day you get up and come to work and deal with other people's problems," she said, unaccountably curious as to what made him tick. She understood people who were motivated by ambition. What motivated Brendan?

"Pretty much." He took a gulp of the soda. "That's what being a minister means. Of course, it also means I get to share their joys."

"Does it balance out?"

He shrugged. "Sometimes."

"You're a fount of information."

He grinned. "Sorry. You're asking me to evaluate my whole ministry in a few words. I don't think I can do it that easily. Can you describe your job that way?"

Could she? "I think so. Basically my job is to help Harvey Gray run the corporation. Anything he wants, I get. Any problem he wants solved, I solve."

"You sound like a guardian angel. I don't suppose you'd like to come work for me, would you?"

"I doubt you could meet the salary requirements."

"Probably not. Is that why you do it? The money?"

"In part." She'd always prided herself on being honest about what drove her. She wouldn't change just because Brendan might think less of her. "Partly it's the challenge. And mostly because it's the way to the top."

"The top of what?"

"The top of the heap." Okay, she didn't know how to explain this to him. "The place where you're the boss. Where no one else can tell you what to do or control you. Ever."

He was looking at her with a sharpening of interest

that made her a little uncomfortable. "That's what you want? To be where no one else can ever control you?"

Why did those particular words come out? "Well, it's more being the boss," she said quickly. "No other woman has ever been where I am with Gray Enterprises. I plan to break a few more traditions before I'm done."

Did he believe her? She wasn't sure. She'd have to be more cautious around Brendan. He had a way of pulling things out that was almost scary.

"Anyway, about Stacy, I wanted to bounce a couple of things off you." Keep the conversation on Stacy, not herself. "She seems to like staying with your aunt and uncle. Do you think that situation is going to last?"

"Probably." The faint lines around his mouth deepened. "Joe and Siobhan have a good record when it comes to taking in strays. They took me in."

"They what?" She looked at him blankly. She'd known he was close to his cousins, but she hadn't known this.

"My parents died when I was thirteen. I went to live with Joe and Siobhan."

"I'm sorry, I know what it's like to lose your parents." Well, her father wasn't dead, but he might as well be, for as little interest as he took in what happened to her.

He nodded, as if accepting that they had something in common, surprising as that was. "Anyway, like I said, they have a good record."

"You weren't a stray." The words were out before she thought he might be offended. "You were a relative."

"It still can't have been easy." His brows knit, and he

seemed to be looking into that past. "They already had five kids, but they made me feel like one of their own. And now they have Seth's little boy. If they can cope with all that, they can handle Stacy."

"I hope so." Much as she hated to admit it, the Flanagan family would probably be good for the girl. "Anyway, Stacy says she wants to get a job, so I can help her with that. Trouble is, she doesn't really have any marketable skills."

"I had a thought about that." He said the words a bit diffidently, as if thinking she wouldn't like an idea if it came from him. "What if we gave Stacy a job helping with the wedding?"

She turned it over in her mind. She wouldn't have expected Brendan to come up something so practical. "That's really not a bad idea." Well, that sounded condescending. Would she ever reach the point that she could just talk to the man in a normal way? "I could certainly use an extra pair of hands, and I don't mind paying for it."

He nodded, apparently not taking offense at her response. "Good. If Stacy's supporting herself, she'll be less likely to fall into old patterns."

Something about his calm assurance annoyed her. "What's going to keep her from going back to Ted the first time he shows up and sweet-talks her?"

Heaven knew, she'd made that mistake often enough.

It'll never happen again, Claire. I swear. I love you. Don't leave me. It'll never happen again.

And it hadn't. Until the next time.

"Nothing will stop her from going back but her own good sense," Brendan said slowly. "However much you or I might want to help her, some decisions she has to make on her own." He leaned forward. Their knees were almost touching, and he took her hand in his, his gaze very intent on her face. "You can't let yourself feel too responsible."

He was a fine one to give that advice, with the responsibility he seemed to feel for everyone around him. "I want to make sure she doesn't get hurt."

"If you make the decisions for her, that's hurting her. That's controlling her, just like Ted tries to do."

"Not with fists."

"But controlling, just the same."

Much as she hated to admit it, he might have a point. "Okay. I guess I get that. How did you get so smart?"

"Painful mistakes, believe me. Some things they can't teach you in seminary. You just have to stumble through on your own." His fingers tightened on hers, and his gaze grew suddenly serious. "I don't want to involve you in anything over your head, Claire. If you need to step back from Stacy, I won't argue."

Here was her chance. All she had to do was say regretfully that she couldn't handle it.

"I'll see it through."

What was she saying? She wanted out, didn't she?

Maybe Brendan's idealism was contagious. Either that, or she just plain couldn't say no to the man.

# Chapter Three

"What on earth are you doing? You'll hurt yourself."

The sound of Brendan's voice startled Claire so much that she nearly slid off the stack of folding tables she'd found in the closet off the church's social rooms. She steadied herself and then turned carefully to look at him. Faded jeans and a gray sweatshirt made him look younger than she knew him to be.

"I won't get hurt unless you scare me into falling. Now you've made me lose count."

"Lose count?" For a moment he looked confused. "Tables? I can tell you how many tables we have. You don't need to kill yourself to find that out." He held out his hand to her. "Come down, please."

"I can get down myself." But when she took a step, the table that had seemed so secure began to slide.

Brendan braced the table with his hip, grabbed her by the waist, and swung her free of the stack. For a moment she leaned against him, her hands on his arms. Her breath caught.

No. No. She didn't feel anything. She straightened, trying to think of something breezy. "You're pretty strong, for a minister."

He let her go, leaning back against the door frame, and gave her a quizzical look. "Is there some rule I'm not aware of that says ministers are supposed to be weak?"

"No." She felt unaccountably embarrassed. "I mean, I don't know. I suppose a strong minister just doesn't fit my image."

"You mean the stereotype of the guy who went into the ministry because he couldn't be successful at anything else? The person who only has to work an hour a week?"

"Something like that." He'd made her feel foolish, and she didn't like that. "I don't know enough about ministers to say whether that's a stereotype or not."

He gave her the look that seemed to probe beneath the surface. "I take it you're not a churchgoer, Claire."

"Me?" She dusted off the knees of her tan slacks. "Not likely."

"Why not?"

The direct question put her on the defensive. "Haven't you ever heard that you're not supposed to ask people about their religion?"

His answering smile was easy, but his eyes were serious. "I'm not interviewing you for a job, so that hardly applies, does it?"

"I don't know why you think it's any of your business, but no, I don't go to church." If he wanted blunt, she could do blunt.

"I'm a minister. We're interested in things like that. Didn't you ever go to church?"

She shrugged, brushing past him. The storage closet was too small for conversation, especially with someone who didn't seem inclined to respect her boundaries.

"I went when I was small. My mother took me. After she died, no one bothered with that." She shrugged. "I haven't ever seen the need for it. Sorry if that's not a polite thing to say to a minister."

"It's honest. I'd rather hear honesty than the excuses some people come up with."

He followed her out of the closet. He was still standing too close, and his gaze was too intent on her face. She'd already decided she wasn't going to let Brendan get that close, hadn't she?

"Well, that's my story," she said briskly. "Now, how many tables did you say you had?"

"Twenty-four, counting the ones in the church school rooms." He accepted the change of subject. "Why do you need to know?"

Maybe she should have mentioned this little problem to Brendan before now. They were supposed to be working together, after all.

"I've been trying all week to find a place for the reception. No luck. We don't have enough time. Everything decent is already booked for that day."

"So you're thinking of having the reception here." He glanced around the social room.

She nodded, frowning at the combination of beige carpet and beige concrete block walls. "It doesn't have the ambience I'd hoped for, but it will have to do. If that's all right with your schedule, that is." He could throw a spanner in the works if it wasn't.

"That's not a problem. What do Gabe and Nolie think about the idea?"

She shrugged. "They want a celebratory meal with family and friends. They don't care where it takes place." She looked around again. "So we'll have to make this room into something special."

"We?"

"You're cooperating with me on the wedding arrangements, remember?"

Although if she were going to follow through on her resolution to stay clear of the Reverend, she ought to let him off the hook, shouldn't she? For a moment the mix of feelings confused her.

She shook her head. "Look, you don't have to do anything. Stacy and I can handle this."

"Oh, I'll help. I don't know how to make centerpieces, if that's what you have in mind."

He'd probably back out if she told him everything she had in mind.

"That's all right. The florist will take care of all that."

"We have a florist?"

"Of course. You can't have a wedding without a florist. Where do you think the bouquet comes from?"

That lock of chestnut hair had fallen on his forehead again, making him look about sixteen. For an instant, her fingers tingled with the impulse to brush it back for him.

"Believe it or not, Nolie and Gabe would be just as married if there were no flowers in sight."

"Maybe so, but they're not going to be. Now, what about folding chairs?"

She spun away. It was safer to look at the expanse of beige carpet rather than Brendan's face.

"Enough for eight at each table, with maybe a dozen extra. We used to have more, but they get borrowed for events and then don't come back."

"That should do." She scribbled the information down in the notebook she'd started with wedding arrangements. After the week she'd had—trying to juggle work, Stacy, and the wedding—if she didn't make notes of everything she'd go crazy.

"Tell me something," Brendan said.

She glanced at him and found he was watching her with a frown.

"What?"

"Why didn't you just ask Siobhan for the information about the tables and chairs? She knows everything there is to know about the church."

She shrugged. "No reason. I didn't want to bother her, that's all." She'd be just as happy if he'd leave that subject alone, but she didn't suppose he would.

"Bother her?" His eyebrows lifted. "I heard her offer to help you with the arrangements."

"Thanks, but I can manage." She snapped the notebook shut.

"Even if you can, that's not the point."

"Of course it is. I'm just doing what Nolie's family would do, if she had any." Why couldn't he let it go? "The groom's family is responsible for putting on the rehearsal dinner, that's all. I don't intend to impose on them for anything else."

"You seem willing enough to enlist me."

He had her there. "Only because you're the one who wanted to make a deal, remember? Besides, you're going to marry them, so you'd be involved to some extent anyway."

"The family wants to help." He had that look again— the one that said he'd keep digging until he understood what made her tick. "Why won't you let them?"

She managed to keep a cool smile on her face. "Because I don't want any help."

"Why?"

Exasperation made her lose her grip on her temper. "You sound like a two-year-old. Why, why, why? Just leave my motives alone and take care of your part of this wedding, Pastor."

Now she was the one who sounded like a two-year-old. In the middle of a tantrum.

But Brendan shrugged, seeming to accept at last that

he wasn't going to get anything else from her. "If that's what you want."

She turned away. His voice stopped her before she'd taken more than a couple of steps.

"But at least you could be honest with yourself about why you need to close out the Flanagan family from planning this wedding."

"Okay, guys, hit the road. I need to lock up."

Brendan held the gym door for the few teenagers who'd hung around to talk after a game of basketball. Claire had been meeting with Stacy this evening, and maybe he had finished in time to talk with her.

Claire had been evasive over the last few days. That was his fault. He'd pushed her too hard the last time they'd talked.

"Why don't you let me have a key, Rev?" Rick Romero leaned against the door, one eyebrow lifted in a challenge. "I'd take good care of it."

"Sorry, Rick. I've lost too many keys that way." He kept his voice friendly, but firm.

"You mean you don't trust us with a key." Rick's expression had darkened, his hair-trigger temper always ready to see offense whether intended or not. The other kids pressed behind him, primed to follow Rick's lead.

"If I didn't trust you, you wouldn't be here at all," Brendan pointed out. He held his breath, knowing the issue could go either way.

Rick glowered for another moment, and the situation

hung in the balance. Then he shrugged, his smile flashing. "Hey, it was worth a try. See you later, Rev."

With a few careless waves, they were gone. He closed the door and locked it, aware as he did so of how futile the gesture was. There were a dozen easy ways into the building if someone really wanted to break in.

He was taking a chance with those kids, walking a tightrope they didn't even know existed. One instance of vandalism or thievery would be enough to bring the church board down on him with both feet.

He switched off the lights and started toward his office. Would Claire stop by? She'd done that several times after meeting with Stacy, staying to share a soda and talk. He'd started looking forward to it.

She probably wouldn't tonight. He thought again of their conversation on Saturday. Ostensibly about the tables, it had ranged a lot further. He'd pushed too much, both about her faith, or lack of it, and her relationship with the rest of the Flanagans.

If Claire had belonged to Jesus as a child, she still did, whether she believed that or not. God would not let go of her easily.

*Father, reawaken Claire to that knowledge of You that she had as a child. I'd like to be Your instrument with her, if that's Your will.*

His worry eased with the prayer. Claire's spiritual well-being was ultimately in God's hands, not his. As for her attitude toward the family—well, he couldn't pretend he understood it, but he'd like to.

His steps quickened. The light was on in his study. Through the open door, he saw Claire sitting in the visitor's chair, the lamplight making her hair glow.

A wave of pleasure swept over him, startling him with its strength. He'd known he wanted to see her. He just hadn't known how much.

"Claire, hi. How did it go tonight?" He tossed his keys onto the desk and swung to face her.

She looked up, and he knew something was wrong. Very wrong.

"What is it?" He reached toward her instinctively. "What's happened?"

"Stacy." Her eyes had darkened with what seemed to be a combination of frustration and anger. "She's pregnant."

He took an involuntary step back and bumped into the desk, struggling to get his mind around the ramifications of that unexpected blow.

"Are you sure?"

"Sure?" She surged out of the chair as if she could no longer be still. The movement brought her close enough that he could smell the spicy scent she wore. "How can I be? Stacy's sure. She says she took three different tests and they all came out positive."

"I guess that's sure enough." He ran his hand through his hair, then gripped the back of his neck. "This complicates things."

"That's putting it mildly."

He wasn't sure whether the edge in her voice was for him, for Stacy, or for the whole situation.

"Honestly, Claire. I never suspected. I'm sorry I got you involved."

"You should be." A bit of dark humor flashed in her eyes. "I thought I was just helping her get a job. I could probably do that, but I'm not qualified for pregnancy counseling."

Something flickered in her face as she said the words, gone so quickly he might have imagined it.

"How is Stacy taking this?"

She shook her head, her hair brushing against her cheek. "What do you think? She's on a roller coaster. One minute she's talking very sensibly about having the baby adopted by a family that can take good care of it. The next, she's indulging in some rosy dream about Ted turning into a model husband and father. As if that's likely to happen."

"Did you tell her that?"

"I suppose you think that was a mistake." Annoyance with him colored her voice. "But Stacy has to face facts. If Ted slapped her around just because he was frustrated about supper being late, he's hardly likely to improve with a baby to take care of."

"They're both so young."

He knew the statistics, only too well. The chance that Ted and Stacy could make a success of marriage, even if that were what both of them wanted, wasn't very good.

"She's agreed to go for counseling with someone qualified to advise her, if I go with her."

He studied Claire's face. In spite of her obvious exasperation, she didn't look as if she intended to bail out at this point.

"Are you sure you want to do that?"

"No." That honesty of hers pleased him. "But I will. Can you set it up?"

He nodded. "I have some names I refer people to. I'll check on who would be the best counselor for Stacy and get back to you. Has she told her mother?"

Claire's expression hardened. "It seems Mom took off on an extended trip with her latest boyfriend. Stacy doesn't even know how to reach her."

"I guess this is up to us, then." Without thinking about it, he reached out and took her hand.

She met his gaze, and hers was serious and steady. "Yes, I guess it is."

They seemed to be making promises to each other—solemn promises that neither could break lightly.

He inhaled, not sure how long it had been since he breathed. His fingers tightened on hers. Irrational as it was, he didn't want to let go.

"All right, then. I'd better tell Ted."

"What?" Claire looked at him as if she couldn't believe her ears.

"Ted," he repeated. "He has to be told."

Had Brendan taken leave of his senses? Claire could only stare at him.

"Why on earth would you think that? Do you want to give him another excuse to knock her around?"

"Of course I don't." Brendan looked taken aback at her vehemence. "But Ted has every right to know he's fathered a child."

"Right?" Her voice rose, and she snatched her hand away from his. What on earth was she doing holding hands with him anyway? "Ted doesn't have any rights. He forfeited them the minute he hit her."

Brendan's gaze didn't waver. "I can understand how you feel, but the law might not see it that way."

She had to make him understand. She couldn't let him put Stacy or the tiny life she carried in jeopardy.

"What if you tell him, and he has a momentary urge to do the right thing and marry her? What if she does?"

"She wouldn't do that."

"She might." *I did.* Her head throbbed with painful memories, battering at her like fists. *I went back. I believed the promises. And I lost my baby as a result.*

The doors of memory were wide open now, and the dark pain came surging over her, blinding her to everything else. The small part of her heart that had never stopped grieving that little life, lost before it could even begin, wept bitter, salty tears.

She took a breath, forcing the memories back. She would not let herself give in to them. They were the past, and she was all about the future.

"Claire? Are you all right?" Brendan was looking at her as if he knew.

No. He couldn't know. No one could.

"I'm fine." She managed to get the words out, managed to detach herself from the pain. It had taken a miscarriage to make her see that he would never change—that she had to get out or die.

She wouldn't let Stacy pay that high of a price if she could prevent it.

"Look." She put some force behind the word. "You're talking about Ted's rights, but it's Stacy we're trying to help here. Stacy is the injured party."

"I know that." Brendan's expression was troubled, his eyes dark and serious.

Hoping he was wavering, she pressed on. "Besides, we don't have the right to tell Ted. That's Stacy's decision to make, not ours."

And she'd do everything in her power to make sure Stacy didn't decide any such thing.

Three vertical frown lines etched themselves between his brows. "I'm counseling Ted. How can I withhold something like this from him?"

She blinked, trying to absorb the words. "You're doing what?"

"I'm counseling Ted." There was a thread of defensiveness in his voice.

She didn't know where to hit first. "You're counseling the abuser. Don't you think that's a conflict? You can't help both of them."

"They both need help."

"Ted is an abuser."

"Ted is also a troubled kid who needs my help. I may not like what he's done, but that doesn't mean I can turn my back on him. My ministry extends to Ted, too."

"Your ministry." She threw the words at him. "What kind of ministry is that? I suppose you think they ought to whitewash everything and get married, just to do the proper thing."

If her words hurt him, he didn't show it. "No, I don't think any such thing. You know that."

She did, but she wouldn't admit it, not when he'd let her down so badly. "You're the one who got me involved with helping Stacy. And all the time you were undercutting what I was doing."

"No, I wasn't." He reached toward her, and she drew back. His hands dropped instantly. "I wouldn't do anything to harm the good you're doing with Stacy."

The pounding in her head had reached mammoth proportions. She'd like to believe him, but she couldn't. And not just because of her own experience.

"That's not true, Brendan. It can't be." The words tasted bitter. "Because if you really believed that, you'd have told me what you were doing."

He stared at her, the color of his eyes almost black. He didn't have an answer. He couldn't, because there wasn't one.

The closeness she'd felt such a short time ago was gone entirely now, replaced by a chasm. Wide and deep and dark.

# *Chapter Four*

Brendan hung up the phone after leaving a message for Claire. It would probably qualify as a miracle if she called him back. The two days since their disastrous exchange about Stacy and Ted had been enough time to kick himself a thousand times about the way he'd handled that situation.

He leaned back, his desk chair squeaking in protest. No use telling himself that he'd been too shocked by the revelation to respond tactfully. If he had that conversation to do over again, he wasn't sure he'd do any better, no matter how much time he had to prepare.

He'd unintentionally burned bridges between them, personal as well as spiritual. She wouldn't forgive him easily.

"Do you have a minute?"

He nearly toppled over backward at the sound of

Claire's voice. He righted his chair. It would probably help not to act like a total idiot just because she was here.

"Of course. Come in." He couldn't help the flood of pleasure at the sight of her, but he could try to contain it so that she wouldn't know. He gestured toward the phone. "I just left a message for you."

And apparently miracles did happen.

"I know." She held up a palm-sized cell phone and then dropped it into the leather bag that was slung from her shoulder. "I'd left the office already, so I thought I'd stop by instead of calling." Her tone was as cool and remote as if he'd called to sell her insurance. "You have some information for me?"

His mind scrambled for the reason he'd called her, swamped by the sheer surprise that she was actually in his office again. Information. Yes, he had that, as well as a suggestion, and both things were going to require a little tact. Correction, a lot.

"I have the counselor's name and phone number here somewhere." He shuffled through the papers that covered his desk, even though he knew exactly where the information was. "Please, have a seat."

Claire hesitated for a fraction of a second, looking at the visitor's chair as if she'd never seen it before. Then she swung her bag off her shoulder and sat down, dropping the bag lightly beside her feet.

Today she wore a pale cream jacket over a green shirt. The combination turned her eyes the same mahogany color as her hair, and she looked cool and elegant in spite of the fact that it was the end of the workday and the June sunshine had brought the outside temperature over eighty.

Focus. Figure out how to approach her about this. Don't let how she looks distract you.

Good advice. Now if he could just manage to take it, he might handle this situation better.

"Here's the counselor's card." He rounded the desk to take it to her. No point in having a piece of furniture between them when he hoped to sway her to his way of looking at things. He sat in the other visitor's chair, watching as she frowned at the card.

"You're convinced this woman is the best person for Stacy? I haven't ever heard of her."

"Would you expect to have heard of her?" It seemed unlikely that someone like Claire would have had any experience of Suffolk's counseling community.

She shrugged. "People talk."

He took a breath, trying to find the right way to phrase what he had to say about the counselor. *Please, Father.*

"I've referred people to her in the past with good results. And the other mental health professionals I've worked with speak highly of her, particularly in the area of pregnancy counseling for teens."

Some emotion flickered in her eyes and was gone. "I guess I'll have to take your word for it."

"There's something else you should know about her." He was walking on eggs, trying to gauge her reaction. "Ms. Fielding is a qualified counselor, but she's also a Christian who counsels according to Christian principles."

Actually, her reaction wasn't that tough to figure out. She stiffened, her fingers tightening on the leather bag strap she still held as if she'd like to swing the purse at him.

"What exactly does that mean? That she shares your concern for the abuser?"

They'd ricocheted right back to their earlier argument. "Beth Fielding will be Stacy's counselor. You don't have to worry about her having a conflict of interest." The words she'd used to him echoed in his head. "I'm sorry you feel as if I do."

Claire's jaw tightened. "It's not a question of how I feel. As long as you're trying to help Ted, you're risking Stacy's well-being."

Was he? He'd struggled with that question since their battle, but he still didn't have an answer.

"Stacy comes first with me," he said carefully. "Her situation is urgent. But I can't ignore Ted's problems. Whether he knows it or not, he needs help, too."

*And you think you're the one to help him.* The voice jeered at him from the back of his mind. *How could you help him? You couldn't even help your own father.*

"Why do you have to be the one to help him?" Claire's question was like an echo. "Why don't you send him to someone else?"

At least he knew the answer to that question. "He wouldn't go to someone else. It's not easy to get these kids to open up to you. They're used to being let down. One mistake and they're gone."

God certainly knew he didn't want to be the one to deal with Ted. Being around the kid only forced him to fight his own inner battle more fiercely.

Claire didn't know that, and her stare was uncompromising. "Isn't it a little arrogant to think you're the only one he'll open up to?"

His temper flared, appalling him. He couldn't let Claire's probing affect him that way. "Maybe so. But at the moment I'm all he's got."

"It seems to me that's all the more reason to get someone else involved."

He had to clench his teeth for an instant before he could speak. Persistence seemed to be Claire's middle name. Was this how his father had felt when his mother went on and on at him about something?

*Please, Lord.*

God knew the rest of that prayer. He'd heard it enough times.

"We seem to be getting off the subject." He nodded to the card she still held in her hand. "We're trying to decide who can best help Stacy, remember? Are you willing to go with her to see Beth Fielding?"

She frowned at the card, her lashes hiding her eyes from him. Finally, she nodded. "I'll give it a try. With one provision."

He was almost afraid to ask what, but she seemed to take his response for granted.

"If I feel this counselor of yours is giving Stacy advice that's against her best interests, we look for someone else."

"Done." A wave of relief swept over him. Claire would recognize Beth's value, he felt sure of that.

"All right. I'll call and set up an appointment. About the cost—"

"The pastor's discretionary fund was set up for things like this." Though how far it would stretch was another question. "I'll handle it."

She nodded. "I guess that's all, then." She started to rise.

"There is one other thing." It was scary how much he'd like her to stay a bit longer. "You said you're trying to help Stacy get a job."

"Trying is the operative word." She brushed a strand of that copper-colored hair back from her cheek impatiently. "Don't schools teach these kids anything about how to get along in the working world?"

"If they do, it doesn't seem to be taking." The faces of his drop-in kids flickered through his mind. "Anyway, I wondered how she responded to the idea of helping with the wedding."

"Not bad. At least she's enthusiastic about it."

"That's half the battle, isn't it?"

She nodded. "I suppose so. I'd like to get her thinking beyond flipping hamburgers for the rest of her life. Maybe that will come."

She stood, picking up her bag.

He rose, too. "If anyone can do it, you can." He touched her arm lightly, wishing he knew how to get back to that feeling that they were in this together. "Believe me, I do have Stacy's best interest at heart. We both do."

She looked at him for a moment, as if measuring the weight of his words. Then she nodded. "I guess I can accept that." She reached for the door.

"I'll see you—"

The door swung open, revealing the kid who waited in the outer office, leaning against the secretary's desk. The last person he wanted to see right now.

"Ted." He tried to sound welcoming. "I didn't expect you."

The boy shrugged, face set in his usual tough-guy mode. "I figured maybe you know where Stacy is."

The outrage that flowed from Claire was almost strong enough to knock him off his feet. He didn't look at her, but he felt it.

"I'm not going to tell you that." He kept his voice even. "But I'd still like to talk to you. Come in."

Ted's fists clenched, but then he shrugged and sauntered through the door.

Brendan glanced at Claire, wanting to tell her—

But Claire was already halfway across the secretary's office, and the very set of her shoulders told him he couldn't say anything to her that she'd be willing to hear right now.

"I still don't see why we have to go to the Flanagan house to do this," Claire said. Three days had passed since that difficult exchange with Brendan, and she still wasn't ready to see him again.

She glanced across the front seat of Nolie's car at her friend. No doubt about it, Nolie looked like a bride-to-be. With her blond hair loose on her shoulders and that contented smile constantly on her lips, Nolie was a poster child for love.

Claire was happy for her. Of course she was. But that didn't mean she wanted to be dragged into such close contact with Nolie's future in-laws.

"We're working on the invitation lists, remember?" Nolie said. "We can't do that without the groom's family."

Nolie had a point, but she didn't intend to admit it.

"They could have just sent me their list. The important thing is to get the text and numbers to the printer."

Nolie braked for a suicidal squirrel dithering in the middle of the residential street. Nolie, with her love of animals, would wait patiently until the creature decided which way it wanted to run.

"We'll do the wording and make up the lists this evening," she said. "Siobhan will be a big help. I still don't understand how you managed to get the printer to agree to do the invitations on such short notice."

"I twisted arms."

Actually, the printer she'd approached did a lot of work for Gray Enterprises. It didn't seem necessary to mention the subtle blackmail she'd applied.

Nolie glanced at her, her blue eyes sparkling with

laughter. "Is that how you're getting Brendan's cooperation, too? Arm wrestling?"

"Pastor Brendan deserves to be body slammed." Nolie and the rest of the Flanagans already knew about Stacy's pregnancy. She could tell her the latest. "He's still trying to counsel the kid who beat up Stacy. I practically tripped on him when I was coming out of Brendan's office the other day."

"Poor Stacy." Sorrow and memory shadowed Nolie's face for a moment. Nolie knew, as well as she did, what abuse felt like. How it could affect the rest of your life even when you thought you were free of it.

Claire shook off the morbid turn her thoughts had taken. That was ridiculous. Nolie was free of the past now, in her love for Gabe. And she herself was free in her success. Neither of them were going back.

"Well, I have to admit Stacy's doing better. And the counselor does seem to be helping, even if Brendan did recommend her."

"Be fair. Brendan isn't a total waste, is he?"

"I refuse to answer on the grounds that you're about to be related to him."

The car turned onto the pleasantly tree-lined street where the Flanagan family lived. It was the kind of street where kids played hide-and-seek outside in the summer twilight. She'd lived on a block like this once, before her mother's death and her father's remarriage had changed her life forever.

Nolie shot her an impish glance as she pulled up in

front of the brick house with the wide, welcoming front porch. "You know, maybe the reason Brendan annoys you so much is that you're too much alike."

"Alike?" She could only echo the word. "What on earth makes you say that?"

"Alike," Nolie said firmly, switching off the ignition. "You're the two most single-minded and determined people I know."

"Love has made you soft in the head if you think I'm anything like Pastor Brendan Flanagan." Claire grasped the door handle. "Let's go in and get this over with. The less time I spend with the Flanagan tribe, the better I'll feel."

"Okay, I think I have everything." Stacy looked up from the lists they'd spread on the Flanagans' oval dining table. "I can put everything on the computer tomorrow."

Claire would like to insist that she could address all those invitations by hand, but that was clearly impossible, given the time limits. The important thing was to get them out, and at least Stacy knew something about using a computer.

"That's great, Stacy." Siobhan, Gabe's mother, gave Stacy a warm smile, and Claire couldn't help noticing how the girl blossomed under the look. "We'll have these ready to be mailed in no time."

"I'll take care of mailing them," Claire said. The Flanagans had helped get the list together, but there was no reason for them to do more.

"We want to help." Siobhan turned that warm smile on her. If she hadn't had her shield in place as usual, she might actually have felt warmed by that look.

"You've already done enough, getting the lists together. To say nothing of the dessert."

There'd been two kinds of pie waiting on the table when she and Nolie arrived, along with coffee and tea. Brendan, Gabe, and Gabe's father had joined them for the dessert, but they'd quickly lost interest when the conversation turned to wedding lists.

Claire could still hear the low rumble of masculine voices from the living room. She thought she could identify Brendan's chuckle.

She dismissed that fancy. They all sounded alike.

And it was just as well the men had wimped out at the thought of making up invitation lists. She had no desire to have Brendan looking over her shoulder while she interacted with his aunt.

Brendan had been completely off base in implying that she had some ulterior motive for excluding the Flanagans from the wedding plans. She was cooperating, wasn't she?

"Now, I've been giving some thought to the shower," Siobhan said.

"You don't need to worry about that. I have it under control."

Her gaze clashed with Siobhan's across the polished table. She'd thought Siobhan was just a soft, fluffy, maternal figure. There seemed to be steel beneath the surface, however.

"I don't want either of you going to that much bother." Nolie's face was troubled. "It's too much work. I don't need a shower."

"Yes, you do," Claire said firmly.

"Of course you do," Siobhan echoed. "Every bride should have a shower. It could be a couples party if you want, but you're definitely having a shower."

"At my place."

She had to get this business back under her control, or the Flanagans would be running everything. Just like Brendan tried to run everything when it came to dealing with Stacy and her troubles.

"We have plenty of room here." Siobhan's gesture swept the dining room and living room.

"My place is big enough."

"Big enough for what?"

Brendan's voice came from close behind her, and a little frisson of awareness swept down her spine. Too close. She wouldn't turn and look.

"We're talking about the bridal shower."

He grasped the top of her chair back, leaning against it casually. "Do the guys get to skip that one?"

Siobhan and Nolie exchanged a laughing glance, as if they'd known he'd say that. The feeling that stabbed her was impossible to mistake. She took a breath, forcing herself to admit the emotion.

Jealousy. She was jealous of Nolie's relationship with Siobhan.

There was nothing pretty about that emotion. She

struggled with the unpalatable truth, while Siobhan and Nolie took turns explaining to Brendan that since it was going to be a couples shower, he couldn't possibly get out of attending.

"All right, all right." He held up his hands in surrender. "Just tell me I don't have to play any goofy games, and I'll be there."

"If there are goofy games, you'll be the first one called on," Nolie promised him.

"You do, and I'll make sure you stumble over your vows," Brendan threatened.

Claire glanced up at his face, then wished she hadn't. She hadn't seen that relaxed, laughing, loving expression before. Maybe that was just as well. It sent a dismayingly strong wave of response sweeping through her.

"You'll behave yourself, Brendan David, that's what you'll do," Siobhan said. "I'll not have Claire thinking I didn't raise you right."

"I'm sure Claire doesn't blame my shortcomings on you."

His smiling gaze challenged her to agree. Maybe it was safest not to respond at all.

"Anyway, about the shower." Siobhan's voice had turned persuasive. "You're doing so much, Claire. At least let us have the shower here. We won't interfere with any arrangements you want to make, but at least we can save you the clutter, and we have plenty of room. Please, won't you let us do that?"

She opened her mouth to refuse, but she caught the

ironic glint in Brendan's eyes and stopped. He knew what was going on with her. He'd recognized that ugly emotion for what it was even before she had.

She certainly wasn't going to give him any more ammunition to use against her.

"Well, if you're sure, it would be lovely to have the shower here." There. That concession would show Brendan how wrong he was.

Unfortunately, he didn't look as if he'd just learned he was wrong. Instead he looked pleased, as if she'd gotten the right answer on a test.

"I can help with that, too." Stacy beamed at the thought of more work, no doubt adding up the hourly wage Claire was paying her.

Claire didn't mind, not when it made the girl look that happy. Stacy's bruises had faded, and she wore a red sweater and an almost-new pair of jeans that she'd confided Gabe's sister, Terry, had given her. Her face had lost its gaunt look, as if just a few days of cherishing by the Flanagan family had made a difference.

"You look as if you like staying here." Brendan seemed to have been thinking along the same lines she had. "And working for Claire."

"Yeah, it's okay." Stacy seemed to feel compelled to dampen her enthusiasm in the face of a direct question. "Claire's showing me how to get ready for a job interview. I'll bet I can get along on my own pretty soon." Her tone wavered, just slightly, on the sentence.

Siobhan covered the girl's hand with a firm clasp.

"We love having you here. You don't have to think about going anywhere until you really want to."

Claire's throat went tight. How much difference would it have made if someone like Siobhan had said that at a crucial point in her life?

"You know, that gives me an idea." Brendan's gaze was suspiciously innocent. "I'll bet there are some other kids at the drop-in center who need to learn how to get ready for a job interview. Maybe Claire could help them, too."

She'd like to say she'd more than fulfilled her end of their bargain by working with Stacy, but she could hardly let the girl know she'd only been helping her because she'd lost in her deal with Brendan.

Besides, that wasn't really the case any longer, anyway. Stacy had become important to her, almost without her noticing it.

"I'm not sure anyone else would be interested in that." She tried to get the subject across in the glare she sent Brendan. He smiled back, unperturbed.

"Sure they would be." Stacy actually sounded excited at the idea, her blasé tone gone. "I could help, too."

"Well." She managed a smile. "I guess we'll do that, then."

"Cool."

"Yes, cool," Brendan echoed Stacy's comment.

He knew exactly how she felt about this. When she got him alone, she'd—

Well, maybe it would be better not to get Brendan

alone at all. She seemed to lose about as many battles as she won with him.

Nolie might have had a point about them, at that. She and Brendan did seem to share something that Nolie, always charitable, had called determination. Someone else might call it just plain stubbornness.

Whatever it was, she didn't think she cared to share it with Brendan.

# *Chapter Five*

"I can't agree to that." Brendan was at his most uncompromising, and Claire's temper flared.

Really, why did the man have to be such an obstructionist? She'd arrived at the church for their meeting with the florist determined to be agreeable if it killed her. It looked as if it might.

She pinned a smile to her face, aware of the florist's interested gaze. "The floral arch is the centerpiece of the floral decorations. Just think how it will frame Gabe and Nolie when they stand in front of you."

She swung toward the florist, who leaned against the front pew, clipboard in hand. "Don't you agree, Ms. Winslow?"

Marge Winslow knew who was paying for the floral decorations. She nodded brightly, happy to provide the expensive piece. "Absolutely. The arch ties the entire theme together."

Brendan didn't seem moved by the florist's enthusiasm. "I'm sorry, but we did agree I'd have veto power on any decorations in the sanctuary."

Claire's good resolutions vanished like ice cream in the June sunshine. Unfortunately, the thought of ice cream just reminded her that she was missing lunch in order to be here in the middle of a workday. She glared at him.

"Why do you have to be so difficult?"

"I'm not." His tense jaw belied the words. "I agreed to the flowers in the windows, on the pews, and on either side of the chancel."

"Well, if you've given in on all that, what difference does the arch make?" She folded her arms across her middle, hoping to suppress any rebellious growl from her stomach.

"The sanctuary is going to look like a flower garden as it is. Don't you think that's enough?" Brendan seemed to be making an effort to sound reasonable, but a muscle twitched irritably in his jaw, suggesting he'd clenched his teeth.

Well, she could be just as stubborn as he could. "Look, can't we resolve this? I don't have much time before I have to get back to work."

Mr. Gray had been surprised, almost affronted, that she didn't intend to work through her lunch hour as she usually did. She'd had to explain where she was going and why, in order to soothe him.

"All the more reason to call it quits," Brendan said. "We have enough flowers."

She planted her hands on her hips. Audience or not, she was going toe-to-toe with Brendan on this. "The arch is an important part of the décor."

"The arch will obstruct the view of the cross."

She blinked. "What?"

He touched her arm, turning her to look at the front of the sanctuary. Deep burgundy drapes hung from a carved wooden pediment, centered with a large gold cross.

"The cross. It's where every eye should be drawn, not toward any individual or any floral display. It's why Gabe and Nolie are being married here, instead of by a judge."

She'd like to argue. She couldn't.

"You could have told me that to begin with. You didn't have to inveigle me into thinking you were just being stubborn."

The annoyance disappeared from Brendan's eyes, and his mouth twitched. "So basically it's my fault that you misjudged me."

"I'd say that's fair." She felt an answering smile curve her lips.

Brendan leaned toward her, and she had the feeling he'd forgotten that the florist stood there. "We could just agree to begin with that I'm always in the wrong. That would save time."

"It would." She couldn't seem to pull her gaze away from his. All that was alive in him sparkled in his eyes when he looked at her that way. She couldn't—

"So, are we having an arch or not?" The florist gestured with her clipboard.

Claire swallowed, taking a step back. Though she was afraid it would take more than a few feet to erase the potency of Brendan's gaze.

"Not," she said.

"Not," Brendan echoed.

Her smile seemed to tangle with his again.

"Okay." The florist turned cool, making some final notes on her sheet. "I'll work this up and get a price list to you later this afternoon."

"Fine." Maybe it was better to focus her attention on the florist. "I'm sure this is going to be beautiful."

"Definitely." The woman shook hands briskly, then scurried toward the side door.

Brendan quirked an eyebrow as the door closed behind her. "Did we scare her off?"

"I'm sure she's dealt with worse." Claire reached for the bag she'd tossed on a front pew. "I've got to get back to work."

"One second." Brendan's hand on her arm stopped her. She looked up at him, and for an instant he seemed to forget whatever it was he wanted to say.

"What? I already agreed with you on the arch."

And the cross. She might not share his beliefs, but she respected them.

"It's not that." He shook his head as he spoke, and that rebellious lock of hair tumbled onto his forehead again, giving him a boyish look that contrasted with the serious expression in his eyes.

"What, then?"

"Have you considered what this is going to cost?" His fingers warmed her through the thin linen of her sleeve. "I'm sure Nolie doesn't expect you to drop a fortune on this wedding."

"It doesn't matter. Really," she added, when he continued to look doubtful. "I don't have anyone else to spend the money on, and it's well worth it to give Nolie a beautiful wedding. I'm not going to count the cost when it comes to my friend's happiness."

His hand slid down to capture her fingers. "You and Nolie have an unusual friendship."

"I guess we do." She didn't intend to say any more about it, but somehow the warmth of his fingers on hers seemed to compel an explanation. "Nolie and I met when we were both at the lowest point of our lives. We helped each other through some rough stuff." He'd never know just how rough.

"That built something strong between you."

She nodded. "That kind of friendship doesn't come along too often in a lifetime."

He gave her that measuring look of his, as if wondering what that low point had been. There was so much sympathy and caring in his eyes that for a moment she almost felt her mouth open, almost felt the rest of the words come rushing out.

No. She drew back, horrified at herself. She couldn't tell him. She didn't tell anyone.

His fingers tightened on hers, almost involuntarily, it seemed. "If you ever want to talk, you know I'm here."

"No. I mean, there's nothing to talk about." She managed a smile, then glanced at her watch.

She didn't have to manufacture an excuse. She was going to be late no matter how she rushed. "I'm late." She grabbed her bag. "I've got to fly."

"Surely, Gray would give you a few extra minutes. You ought to get something to eat."

"He would, but I'm not going to ask."

Brendan didn't understand, and she didn't bother trying to explain. If she started asking for special favors, she'd put herself in a position of weakness, and there were several people who'd be only too happy to take advantage of that.

"I'll see you later." She bolted out the door.

No, Brendan didn't understand. His job was a safe cocoon. Hers was a battle, where the weak got eaten. Somebody like Brendan could never understand that.


"No, no. Don't look down at the floor. Look at the interviewer."

Claire sounded exasperated. Brendan really couldn't blame her. She hadn't wanted to work with the other teens, and he knew she'd only agreed to this evening's session because Stacy cared.

He glanced at his watch. He'd never have believed it could take over an hour just to get the approach to the interviewer and the handshake right. Unfortunately, his drop-in kids had a long way to go.

He shifted restlessly on the metal folding chair. The

gym hadn't seemed like the right setting for Claire's work with the kids on job-interview tactics, so he'd moved them to Fellowship Hall. Unfortunately, that brought them into an area where they were far more likely to encounter other people.

So far, so good, though. No one had come in.

Right now Claire had one kid playing the role of the interviewer, sitting behind a table, while the others took turns coming up to the "desk," introducing themselves, and shaking hands.

"Okay, not bad." Claire finally let Gin Carter off the hook, and the girl slumped into a chair with relief. "Who's next?"

Rick Romero, who'd been sitting in the back and making comments sotto voce throughout the hour, stood and sauntered to the front. "Take me, Teach."

Rick's words were just short of an insult, and Brendan tensed. Maybe this hadn't been such a great idea after all. Claire probably didn't encounter many Rick Romeros in her everyday life.

"All right, let's see what you've learned." Claire's voice was crisp and businesslike. "I'll take over as interviewer." She slid into the seat behind the table.

Rick made a play of knocking on an imaginary door, raising a laugh and a few jeers. Then he slouched toward the table.

Claire didn't let him get more than a few feet. "Stop right there."

Instead of halting, Rick swaggered to the table and

leaned across it toward Claire. "So, am I making an impression on the boss?"

Brendan's muscles tightened. If he had to intervene, it would be bad for all of them.

Claire leaned back in her chair, her gaze so cool as to be almost insulting as she swept it over the boy. "You're making an impression, all right."

Rick smirked, leaning closer.

"A bad one," she went on, voice dispassionate. "Everything about the way you approached the interviewer said you didn't care about the job. You've already told the interviewer it's a waste of time even to talk to you."

Quick anger flared in Rick's face. "Don't you disrespect me like that."

Claire stood, leaning forward until her face was inches from Rick's. "Then don't you disrespect me."

He held his breath. He'd never have gotten right in the kid's face like that, but Claire held her own. Any sign of fear and it would have been all over, but she wasn't afraid. As far as he could tell, she wasn't afraid of anything.

Rick glared back, hands clenched. Then his expression eased, and he shrugged.

Brendan let his breath out and then shoved back his chair. "Why don't we take a break now? Cider and doughnuts are on the kitchen pass-through. Help yourselves."

Any tension that was left in the room dissolved as kids surged toward the food. Teenagers always seemed to be hungry, especially these kids. Sometimes he wondered when, or if, they actually had a normal meal.

He caught up with Stacy as she headed for the line. No matter what else was wrong, at least she had lost that bedraggled-kitten look she'd worn since he met her. Nobody ever lacked for either food or love in the Flanagan house, that was for sure.

"How's it going, Stacy?"

"Claire was great, wasn't she?" Her voice was hushed with admiration.

"She was." He certainly couldn't argue with that.

"She always looks so great, too." Stacy's gaze lingered on Claire, who stood talking to one of her earlier victims.

Claire gestured as she made some point, the silver bangle on her wrist catching the light. She'd arrived in the same work clothes she'd had on earlier in the day— a deceptively simple gray suit and silk shirt—either because she'd wanted to impress the kids with proper attire or because she hadn't had time to change. No matter what she wore, she always looked perfectly put together.

Stacy shot a look at him, as if he'd argued the point. "She does, doesn't she?"

"Definitely." He smiled at her.

She didn't return the smile. "She looks like she belongs." Stacy's voice dropped, and her shoulders slumped. "I'll never look like that."

Her pain grabbed his heart. He touched her shoulder lightly. "You can if you want it, Stacy. I'm sure Claire would tell you that. But whether you do or not, you're still precious in God's sight. And mine. And a lot of other people's. You have friends, don't forget."

Her shoulders straightened a little at that. "Yeah, I guess I do."

She went on toward the doughnut counter, a little more life in her step.

It was easy enough to reassure Stacy. It wasn't so easy to reassure himself. As welcome as she was, Stacy couldn't stay with Aunt Siobhan and Uncle Joe forever. What was next for her? He had to talk with Claire about how the counseling was going.

"Why are you wearing that worried frown?" Claire sipped at a plastic cup of coffee, instead of indulging in cider and doughnuts. "If you're not happy with the session, I'd be glad to quit."

"No chance," he said quickly. "You're doing a great job. Even under pressure."

She shrugged. "He's not as tough as he thinks he is. Although I'd hate to guarantee a job for that one."

"There are no guarantees, in any event." He shook his head, his gaze on Stacy as she joined a couple of her girlfriends. "I was thinking about Stacy, as a matter of fact. Praying that the right thing is going to open up for her."

"I'm not a great believer in waiting for the right thing to come along. If Stacy wants a better life, she'll have to go after it."

He switched his gaze to Claire. "That sounds a little cold-blooded."

She shrugged. "That's me. I'm told they call me the Dragon Lady behind my back at work."

"Seeing you with Stacy, I find that hard to believe." And with Nolie, for that matter. Claire lost all her sharp edges when she was with her friend.

"I sympathize with her. I'm willing to help her." There was a thread of defensiveness in her voice. "I just know the determination has to come from her."

How do you know that, Claire? He didn't think she'd welcome that kind of probing question now, maybe not ever. Still, she'd revealed a little something about herself when she'd talked about her bond with Nolie. She was probably regretting that now.

What had that low point of her life been? It was hard to imagine, looking at the polished, successful woman she was today, that it could have been anything very serious.

"I grant you, the pregnancy has made Stacy wake up and get a grip." Claire apparently felt he'd been silent in disagreement. She let her gaze rove over the gaggle of teens. "I'm not sure anything short of that would jolt the rest of them enough to make a difference. They're drifting, and they don't care enough to swim against the current."

"Maybe so." He wished he could make her see what he saw when he looked at that gang of kids. "But there's so much potential there. They're not dumb. They could have good, productive lives." He leaned toward her, intent on making her understand.

But the coolness didn't leave her eyes. "That's what you want, Pastor. Not necessarily what they want."

"They've got it in them," he persisted, not sure why it mattered what Claire thought about his pet project.

"At the moment, it looks like all they've got in them is trouble."

He followed the direction of her gaze. One of the kids had tossed a wadded-up napkin at Rick. He swung around instantly, fury darkening his eyes. Before Brendan could move, Rick threw his glass straight at the kid.

The glass shattered against the door, sending shards of glass flying and spattering cider on the carpet. There was a moment of frozen silence in which no one moved.

Then the door swung open. Harvey Gray stood there.

Brendan heard a sharp gasp from Claire, reminding him that Harvey was her boss. He didn't need any reminding that, as a member of the church council, Harvey was also one of his bosses.

And at the moment, Harvey didn't look as if he cared much for either of them.

Claire's stomach lurched unpleasantly. She couldn't imagine what Harvey Gray was doing there, but it couldn't be good. Harvey ran a tight ship. He wasn't one to think teenage horseplay was normal or acceptable, even if the teens involved had been members of his church.

And what would he feel about his trusted lieutenant being a part of it? She didn't even want to think about that.

"Mr. Gray." She took a step forward, trying to sound as if it were normal to meet him in the church's Fellowship Hall with a group of unruly street kids in attendance.

Gray didn't even bother to acknowledge her greeting. He turned toward Brendan, his piercing blue eyes focused on the pastor; his tall, attenuated figure, likened by the office wits to a bald stork, held stiff and tense.

"Pastor, what is the meaning of this?"

Brendan smiled, looking as relaxed as if it had been Gabe who'd come through the door instead of a prickly, influential member of his governing board. "I didn't expect to see you tonight, Harvey. We're having a job-training seminar this evening."

Gray's gaze swept over the group, then moved to the broken glass and sticky stains. "I see. When did job training include damage to church property?"

Of course, that was the first thing he'd focus on. Gray was obsessed with the value of property. He'd undoubtedly put the safety of the church building ahead of any other considerations.

Be careful, Brendan. Be careful.

"Just a little accident with the refreshments," Brendan said easily. "No harm done."

No, no. That was exactly the wrong approach to take with Gray. Brendan should never belittle his concerns.

Sure enough, Gray stiffened, drawing more erect and strengthening the resemblance to a stork. She had to stifle a nervous laugh. This wasn't a laughing matter, although Brendan didn't seem to realize that.

"It looks to me as if a great deal of harm has been done." He pointed. "Who will pay for cleaning the carpet?"

"I'm sure a little spot cleaner will get that stain right up." Brendan still didn't give the impression that he took Gray seriously.

Gray's pale, cold gaze inspected the group of teenagers. Several of them shifted nervously from foot to foot, although Rick stood and glared. They saw trouble, if Brendan didn't.

"Who are these people, Pastor? I don't recognize any members of our church here."

"No. These are some of the kids from the neighborhood who drop in to play basketball now and then. Claire was kind enough to agree to do a job-application session with them."

Don't do me the favor of drawing attention to me. But it was too late. It had been from the moment Gray walked in.

He hadn't questioned her about why she was there. That wasn't his way. But he was putting a mark against her in that mental ledger he kept on everyone who worked for him.

"I assume the session is now over." His tone made it clear it had better be.

"Well, no, we were just taking a break."

Brendan was being remarkably obtuse when it came to relating to someone as influential as Harvey Gray. Agree with him, she wanted to shriek. Just agree with him.

Luckily, the kids seemed to recognize what Brendan

didn't. They were already filtering out the back door, some of the braver pausing long enough to snatch up a few more doughnuts from the boxes.

Brendan shrugged. "I guess we are finished for the night."

"I'd suggest that you're finished for good." Gray's tone was silky.

Agree, she cried silently. Just agree.

Brendan's jaw tightened, as if he finally got it. "No, I don't think so."

"Brendan," she began, but neither of them seemed to be paying any attention to her.

"And I don't think the board is aware of these extra-curricular activities of yours with a bunch of hoodlums."

Claire heard, only too well, the undertone of menace in the words.

"That fact that they don't belong to the church doesn't make them hoodlums. Or gangbangers." She could feel Brendan's tension as surely as if she'd been touching him instead of standing several feet away. "I see them as part of my ministry here."

Gray seemed to weigh the words. Then he nodded slowly. "I see. In that case, we may need to evaluate just what your ministry is."

Sending a last, disdainful look at the stain on the carpet, Gray turned and stalked out of the room. The door swung shut behind him.

Brendan frowned at the closed door for a long moment. Finally he shrugged, turning to her. "I'm sorry that disruption cut your session short tonight. We'll have to schedule another time."

She could only stare at him. Did he really not understand what was at stake?

"Tell me something, Brendan. When is your contract here up for renewal?

For an instant he stared at her blankly. "In the spring. But you don't think—"

"He was threatening you." A wave of anger swept over her. "Are you too naive to realize that?"

"Of course he wasn't threatening me. You're overreacting. Sure, he's upset about the stain on the carpet, but he'll get over it."

"It's not the stain on the carpet that's getting to him. It's you. Employees don't defy Harvey Gray without consequences."

Brendan stiffened, as if she were the enemy, not Harvey Gray. "The man is on my church board. That doesn't make me his employee."

"I suppose you think you're employed by God." How could he be so oblivious to the danger a man like Gray represented?

"In a way." Brendan was looking at her as if she were a stranger.

Maybe she was.

"Well, I am employed by Gray. And believe me, if he's taking you down, I don't intend to go with you."

## Chapter Six

Brendan jabbed the punching bag repeatedly, finding the rhythm and the effort soothing. He'd hung the bag in the corner of the gym during his first month here. He hadn't used it much at first, but he'd been finding reason to more and more often in recent months.

It was ironic, in a way, that the person who spent so much time breaking up fights between the kids had to take out his own frustrations on the bag. The teens probably saw him as some do-gooder who never got angry. If they knew the truth about who he was inside—

Well, hitting the bag was better than any alternative he could come up with. Uncle Joe had put the gloves on him when he was fourteen or so, rightly feeling that a kid who'd seen the worst use of fists ought to learn a better way.

Sweat soaked into his T-shirt, but he didn't stop. He had a lot to work out today. His frustrations with the kids, who hadn't responded in the way he'd hoped to what Claire tried to teach them, had been compounded by that unpleasant encounter with Harvey Gray.

And then there'd been Claire's reaction. He frowned, letting his rhythm slow. She'd been angry with him, acting as if he were some totally naive idiot who didn't know a thing about the world.

Could Claire really believe that one of his parishioners would embark on a campaign against him because of a simple disagreement? That was ridiculous.

"Are you angry with someone, by any chance?"

He must be having some sort of auditory hallucination. That couldn't possibly be Claire's voice.

He stopped the bag and turned. She stood in the gym doorway, looking too pristine in her pale beige pantsuit to venture inside the room. Her bronze hair curved around her face like the petals of a chrysanthemum, and her creamy skin begged to be touched.

Well, he'd better stop that line of thought right now.

"No." He shrugged. "Well, hitting the bag is a way of taking out my frustrations, but I didn't have anyone in particular in mind."

"Then you're missing a great opportunity." She came toward him then, skirting the hand weights that lay on the dusty floor. The custodian must have been skipping this part of the church in his cleaning routine.

He pulled off the gloves. "I didn't expect to see you here today." Or ever, for that matter.

"No, I guess not." Her gaze evaded his.

He grabbed a towel, trying to clean up the best he could. What he needed was a shower, but he could hardly ask Claire to wait around while he made himself presentable.

He mopped his face. "So, are you going to tell me what brought you, or do I have to guess?"

She shot him an annoyed look. "All right. I came to apologize."

He blinked. "For what?"

"I shouldn't have interfered in your relationship with Harvey Gray. It's not any of my business."

He hadn't expected that, given how strongly she'd seemed to feel the night before. Had she changed her mind? Or just decided it was safer to stay out of the situation?

"Harvey's your boss." He trod carefully, wondering what she was thinking. "You probably know him a lot better than I do. You don't have to apologize for trying to give me what you feel is good advice."

"Advice you don't intend to take."

"Claire—" He hesitated, not sure what to say. "Look, I just think you overreacted a little. My relationship with a parishioner is a lot more complex than your relationship with your boss."

He could read the skepticism in her eyes. She didn't believe that.

"Maybe you're right," she said carefully. "I don't think so, but as I said, it's not my business."

"And you want to stay out of it, right?"

Her gaze cooled. "I think it would be best if my work didn't get tangled up with my personal life."

"Fair enough." He could respect that. "I hope what happened last night didn't cause any unpleasantness for you at the office."

For the first time since she'd come in, a faint smile touched her lips. "Oddly enough, there was a small crisis at the office this morning. Mr. Gray found that distracting enough to keep his mind off whatever I might be doing in my spare time."

He didn't know quite how to react to that. "Are you saying you manufactured something just to keep his mind off last night?" If so, Claire was a lot more devious than he'd imagined.

"Not manufactured, no." She looked a little offended at that. "Believe me, I never have to manufacture crises. There's always something. It's just that usually I solve them without involving Mr. Gray."

"But today you let him deal with it."

"This morning I let him know it existed," she corrected. "This afternoon I'll take care of it. He'll be grateful, and the subject of my involvement with your juvenile delinquents won't come up."

"Devious."

"You don't approve." She was nearly as quick to take offense as Rick.

"I'm not criticizing. I just don't agree with manipulating people."

"Then it's a good thing you're not in the business world, Pastor."

"Maybe so."

*Father, she's angry at my words, but maybe that's a good thing. Maybe it will make her think twice about how she relates to people.*

Claire's lips tightened. "Just take care of your parishioner, then, and let me deal with my boss in my own way. And if you're talking with him about those kids, please leave my involvement out of the conversation. Hopefully he'll think my presence last night was strictly a one-shot deal."

"Does that mean you're backing out on helping Stacy?" He frowned.

She gave an exasperated sigh. "Of course not. I just mean that Harvey Gray doesn't have to know I'm doing it."

"I certainly won't go out of my way to tell him, but I can't lie about it." Didn't she see that would be wrong, to say nothing of the damage it would do to his relationship with a member of the congregation?

She seemed to be gritting her teeth. "Can you avoid the subject entirely, then?"

"Fine. I'll do my best."

He certainly didn't have any burning desire to talk with Harvey about his work with the teens. The previous night's events had just made it clearer that he should keep his ministry to the kids separate from his congregation.

"That'll have to do." She snapped the words and turned toward the door.

"Claire."

She stopped. "What?"

"Thank you for coming by to apologize. I appreciate it."

She looked as if she were struggling to keep from biting his head off. "Fine," she said, grinding the word out. "I've got to go."

He found himself grinning as the door slammed behind her. Claire might insist that she didn't care a thing about him and his work. She could declare that she didn't have an idealistic bone in her body and that she was only working with Stacy because of that silly bargain with him.

But he knew better. The very fact that she'd come today told him that God was starting to work on Claire, whether she realized it or not.

"I didn't realize Brendan would be here tonight."

Claire hesitated in the doorway, wishing back the words as soon as she spoke them. There was certainly no reason to betray to Siobhan Flanagan, of all people, that she had any interest in Brendan.

Which she didn't, she hastened to assure herself. She was surprised, that's all. He hadn't mentioned he was coming to the Flanagan house for the shower-planning meeting.

Siobhan took her arm, leading her into the shabby living room with a smile. "Brendan shows up to have supper with us whenever he can. We like having the family together around the table."

It was shabby, she thought again, glancing around the living room. The furniture had seen better days, and the coffee table bore the scars only a large family or a college fraternity would inflict. She compared it mentally with her own elegant, virtually untouched living room.

Untouched. She felt the smallest bit of uneasiness.

The Flanagan living room had seen actual living. Every surface was crowded with family photos and memorabilia. The whole history of a family was encapsulated in this space. They probably felt that was worth a few nicks and scars.

"Supper will be ready in a few minutes." Siobhan gestured toward a chair. "Relax. And don't worry— we'll get rid of some of the males before we start the shower planning."

Ryan, the youngest of the Flanagan brothers, looked up from the carpet where he was playing with Seth's little boy. He grinned. "You won't have to ask me twice, Mom. I don't know a thing about showers, and I don't plan to learn."

Brendan leaned forward in his easy chair to tap him lightly with the newspaper he held. "Maybe you ought to learn, Ry. Some woman will trip you up one of these days."

"Not me." Ryan shook his head, a lock of Irish black hair falling on his forehead. "I'm having too much fun to hit the matrimonial trail."

Nolie had told her that Ryan had a good heart behind all that charming exterior. She'd have to take her word for it. Funny, that the Flanagan men looked so alike but were so different in personality.

Brendan sent a smile her way. "Don't worry. I don't have any opinions on showers."

"Then that must be the only topic you don't have an opinion on."

He held up both hands in surrender, the lines crinkling at the corners of his eyes. "Truce, please."

That smile had a way of getting under her skin, and the realization made her guard go up. At least Brendan was fully dressed now, in a pair of khakis and a deep blue Polo shirt. When she'd found him working out in shorts and a T-shirt, she'd let herself dwell a lot more than she should have on the breadth of his shoulders and the long lines of his body.

Off-limits, she reminded herself. She didn't intend to get involved with anyone, and if she did, it certainly wouldn't be with a stubborn, opinionated minister.

"Isn't Stacy here?" She glanced toward the kitchen. The girl might be helping Siobhan. "I wanted to hear how her job interview went."

Brendan got up and came toward her. "Now, don't overreact."

Tension rippled along her nerves. "What happened? How can I overreact when I don't know what's going on? Where is she?"

"She's upstairs." Brendan's fingers closed around

her wrist. "I'll take you up, but she wanted me to talk to you first. She ditched the interview."

Behind him, Joe and Ryan had begun a conversation, no doubt designed to show that they weren't listening. She lowered her voice anyway.

"Ditched. She didn't go at all?" I set it up for her, she wanted to say, but that was hardly the point.

"She panicked at the last minute and didn't go in." His grasp tightened. "Listen, don't blow up at her."

That annoyed her more than Stacy's actions. "Do I look as if I intend to blow up?"

"You look irritated."

She took a deep breath. "That's at you, not Stacy. Can I see her now?"

He led her to the stairs. "Come on up. She's staying in my old room, as it happens."

She preceded him up the carpeted steps, running her hand along a railing made smooth by generations of hands. Stacy had fallen into a family.

The thought startled her. She'd been thinking that Stacy was lucky to have a safe place to stay, but the Flanagan house was more than that.

The upstairs hall sported faded floral wallpaper and an equally faded carpet. The door with train decals must have belonged to Seth's little boy. Brendan rapped on a white-paneled door on the right.

"Stacy? We want to talk, okay?"

"Come in." Stacy's voice sounded as if it were clogged with tears.

He opened the door on a twin-bedded room, its walls hung with posters a decade out-of-date. Bookcases jammed with books surrounded a window that looked out over the tree-shaded back lawn.

Stacy was slumped on one of the beds, clutching a pillow. Her eyes were red and puffy, and the sight wrenched Claire's heart, wiping out whatever she might have been going to say.

"Hey, Stacy." She touched the girl's shoulder lightly. "It's all right. I'm not mad at you."

The girl sniffled, her long hair hanging down to hide her face. "You went to all that trouble for me, and then I blew it."

Brendan sat on the other twin bed, its old-fashioned metal springs creaking in protest. "We've all blown it a few times. Why should you be any different?"

"That's right." She sank onto the bed next to Stacy. She'd expected sympathy from Brendan, but his easy empathy surprised her a little. "Brendan's right. We've all missed opportunities. There'll be another one."

"You won't want to help me again."

Two weeks ago that would have been true. She'd have given the girl one chance to get her act together, and then she'd have moved on.

Something had changed. Was she losing her edge?

"Of course I want to help you." She put her arm around Stacy's shoulders. "We'll find the right job for you, you'll see. And next time I'll go along with you to the interview, okay?"

"You will?" Stacy's tears spilled over again.

"Only if you stop crying." She gave the girl a hug. "You go wash your face for supper. Tomorrow we'll start looking for another job. Okay?"

The smile sparkled through Stacy's tears like a rainbow. "Thanks, Claire. I won't let you down again. I promise." She scrambled to her feet, brushing away tears. "I'll go get ready for supper." She hurried out of the room.

Brendan looked at her. "Nice job," he said softly.

"You, too."

Their knees were almost touching, and the smile he gave her was secret, almost intimate. She was way too aware of his presence in the quiet room. She glanced around, seeking something to break the spell.

"Looks as if you had pretty eclectic tastes in music." She nodded toward the rock-group poster that hung next to an ad for a performance of Carmen at the opera house.

"Aunt Siobhan's influence battled that of the other kids." He grinned. "She made sure we were all exposed to the classics, whether we liked it or not." He moved slightly, and his knee brushed hers. "What about you? Did you take piano lessons, violin—what?"

"My mother taught me to play the piano. Well, tried to teach me, anyway." She had a brief image of her small hands next to her mother's on the piano keys. "But after she died, my father got rid of the piano, so I didn't keep up with the lessons."

"That's too bad." His voice had the same warm, empathetic tone he'd used with Stacy. "Maybe he couldn't handle the reminders of her."

"Maybe." And maybe she'd exposed too much of her personal side to Brendan. She didn't waste time thinking of the past, let alone talking about it to anyone.

She stood up, deliberately breaking the link between them. "Your Aunt Siobhan probably has supper ready. We'd better go down."

Brendan nodded, getting up, too. "Sure." He sounded just as cool and agreeable as she might wish.

But there was a warmth and caring in his eyes that she didn't want to see there. That she could only hope wasn't reflected in her own.


"If we could have a little silence from the living room, we'd probably be done faster," Siobhan called, in a voice meant to be heard by the men, who'd retreated to the living room after supper, leaving the shower planners seated around the dining room table.

That was a good idea in theory. Unfortunately, they kept hearing ridiculous suggestions coming from the other room.

"Ignore them. You know the more attention you pay, the worse they'll be."

Mary Kate, the oldest of the Flanagan clan, had left her children with a sitter since her husband, Kenny, also a firefighter, was on duty, as was Seth. She'd breezed in after supper, red curls flying, not looking old enough to have two children.

"If you think you can outwit Ryan by ignoring him, you haven't been around lately. Honestly, sometimes you'd think he was still a kid." Terry, the sister who was two years older than Ryan, had the same red curls.

Claire made a valiant effort to keep the siblings straight. Terry was a paramedic with the fire department. As Joe had said, everyone followed the family tradition.

"Well, I think we've finished most of it, anyway," she said, glancing at the notes Stacy had been taking. "Thanks to all of you."

She could only hope there wasn't an edge to her smile as she looked at the Flanagan women. She appreciated their help—of course she did. It was just hard to keep their enthusiasm from sweeping the wedding shower totally out of her control.

"Believe me, I've attended way too many showers lately," Terry commented. "It seems like everyone I know is getting married."

"Maybe that's a hint," Mary Kate said.

Terry threw a wadded-up napkin at her older sister. "Listen, just because you're an advertisement for marriage and family, don't try to push me into it. I'm busy enough with my career."

"You can have a job and be married. You just have to make the time to date someone." Mary Kate's eyes took on a calculating look. "There's this friend of Kenny's cousin we could introduce you to."

"Forget it. I've met Kenny's cousin. He couldn't possibly have a friend I'd like."

Siobhan watched the good-natured bantering with a soft smile, clearly enjoying the girl-talk.

Was this what her life would have been like if her mother had lived? Would she have been planning things with her, sitting at a table exchanging woman-talk and laughing gently? A longing she hadn't experienced in years swept over her, and to her horror she actually felt tears sting her eyes.

There was no point in thinking about what might have been.

Besides, that wasn't what she wanted any longer. She didn't yearn for family life, hadn't since she was a teenager, in any event. All she wanted was professional success. If her connection to the Flanagans threatened that, she'd cut them off without a backward glance.

"Enough, girls." Siobhan's gentle scolding suggested that Mary Kate and Terry were about six or seven. "We've gotten through everything on my list, I think. Claire, is there anything we've forgotten?"

"I can't imagine what," she said. "This ought to be the best couples shower Suffolk has ever seen. We just have to make sure Nolie and Gabe show up on time."

"We'll put Brendan in charge of that," Terry said, then jerked when her beeper went off.

At almost the same moment, Claire heard a beeper from the other room. Brendan's, she realized, as he beat Terry to the phone.

The occupants of both rooms seemed to freeze as everyone listened to his end of a monosyllabic conversation. He hung up and then turned to them with an expression Claire hadn't seen on his face before.

"Down at those new apartments on Fourteenth Street." He seemed to be speaking a language everyone understood but her. "Looks like it's going to be at least three alarms."

Terry was already headed for the door, with Ryan on her heels. Brendan, eyes abstracted, followed them.

He was praying, she realized, and didn't know how she knew that.

"Ryan, you're not on call," Siobhan said, a faint protest in her voice.

Ryan glanced at her. "They'll call everyone for a building like that. I might as well beat them to it."

Joe got up, too. "I'll just drive by and see how the scene looks." He came to bend over Siobhan and drop a kiss on her cheek. "Don't worry. You know they won't let me near the action."

She nodded, her mouth tight, and reached up to pat his cheek. "I better not hear about any Flanagans taking foolish chances," she said.

They went out, one after the other. No fuss, no hurry, but they were gone in two minutes flat.

Once the door clicked closed, Mary Kate got up, gathering her notes and her bag. "I'd better get home, Mom. I don't trust that sitter not to scare the kids by turning the television on to news about the fire."

Siobhan gave her a quick hug. "Call me later."

In a moment the house that had seemed so full felt

empty. Stacy rose, looking as if she didn't understand, but knew this wasn't good. "I'll go put the rest of the dishes away."

"You don't need to," Siobhan began, but the girl had already disappeared into the kitchen. Siobhan shrugged, looking at Claire. "Poor child. She's picking up on my tension, I suppose."

"It's natural enough." Claire sought a neutral tone. "Is it always like that? All of them going?"

She'd known, intellectually, that they were all involved with the fire department. She just hadn't thought through what that meant.

"For something big it is." Siobhan clasped her hands together on the table. "The good Lord knows I should be used to it after all these years, but I'm not. I'm ashamed to admit I'm almost glad Gabe's injury took him out of it."

"I don't think you need to be ashamed of that. At least one of them isn't in danger right now. Although I suppose Brendan, since he's the chaplain, doesn't—"

Siobhan shook her head, stopping that line of thought. "Brendan will be in the thick of it, too. Minister or not, he's trained and he never can hold back." She reached out and clasped Claire's hand. "You must know him well enough by now to know that."

She wanted to protest that she barely knew Brendan, but she couldn't. Siobhan was right—Brendan wouldn't hold back on what he thought was his duty, just because it was dangerous.

"No, I guess he'll rush right in and take responsibility, won't he?"

Siobhan nodded, hand still grasping Claire's. "He's been that way since he came to live with us. Always carrying a load of responsibility for everyone he meets. I don't expect he'll ever change."

"Even if it gets him into trouble?" She thought of Harvey Gray.

"Even then." Siobhan studied her. "You're thinking of his set-to with Harvey Gray and those teenagers, aren't you?"

She probably shouldn't discuss it with Siobhan, but somehow she needed to. "He doesn't seem to realize how dangerous a man like Gray can be. He shouldn't make an enemy of him."

"No, Brendan wouldn't realize that. He's an idealist, and he always feels as if he has to carry the weight of the world on his shoulders."

Yes. That was exactly what she'd sensed about him.

"His parents did that to him," Siobhan added softly, almost as if thinking it to herself. She shook her head. "He shouldn't be trying to do everything at the church by himself. Nobody can do that. It's not good for him or for the members."

She wasn't sure what Siobhan meant, but at least she seemed to agree with Claire's assessment. "Can't you tell him that? Tell him not to make an enemy of someone like Gray." Brendan's parish politics shouldn't matter to her as much as it did.

"I've tried. I think he'll have to come to that himself. He's not one to listen."

"Stubborn," Claire said.

"Oh, yes. Like all of them." Siobhan's smile lingered for a moment, then faded. Her fingers tightened on Claire's. "Will you pray with me?"

"I don't think—" Everything in her cringed away from the suggestion.

"For their safety. Please."

She could hardly refuse, could she? She nodded, bowing her head, hoping fervently that Siobhan didn't expect her to say anything.

"They're out on the line again, Father." Siobhan's tone was quiet, almost conversational. "You know what it's like there. Be with them as they do what must be done. Protect those in danger. Please, bring our loved ones home safely to us."

The lump that formed in Claire's throat wouldn't have allowed her to say anything if she had wanted to. They're not my loved ones, she ought to protest, but maybe that wasn't even true. She knew them. She cared what happened to them.

They seemed to move through her mind, almost as if she held them up for some sort of blessing. Joe, who was supposed to be confined to a desk job since his heart attack. Seth, the single dad who seemed to be everyone's best friend. Kenny, Mary Katherine's husband. Terry, with her lively, determined manner and her skilled hands. Ryan, the charmer with the quick smile. And Brendan.

What about Brendan? Her mind and heart seemed to be arguing with each other. Her mind said that Brendan didn't mean anything to her, and that she didn't believe in prayer even if he did.

Meanwhile her heart had launched into a silent plea. *Keep him safe.* She didn't know who she spoke to. *Keep him safe.*

## Chapter Seven

Brendan paused on the brick sidewalk, glancing down the cobblestone street at the stalls set up on either side. After spending the previous evening at a smoky fire, trying to comfort people who'd just seen most of their possessions burned to a crisp, it was good to stand in the clear sunlight and inhale the lush aromas of the farmers' market.

There'd been plenty of property lost, but no loss of life, thank God. The situation had been the usual odd mix of heroism and selfishness—he ought to be used to that by now. Some people risked their lives for those in need, while others raged at God for their losses.

Some threatened to sue anyone and everyone they could think of. He'd seen one man brush off Terry's offer of care while declaring he'd sue the fire department for not getting his new television out of the burning building.

Terry had met his eyes and shrugged—hers were red-rimmed from smoke. She knew as well as he did how people could be. Shock could do strange things, of course, but he had a feeling that it was in the crises of life that a person's soul showed through in the most unguarded way.

He wandered down the row of stalls, keeping an eye open for any early raspberries. One of his favorite parishioners, Mike Snow, had lost his sight and his mobility, but he still loved to eat, and red raspberries were a particular favorite. He'd love to drop some off at the nursing home and see the expression on Mike's face when he smelled them.

Claire had been gone when he got back to the Flanagan house after the fire. That hadn't been surprising, but the news that Claire had joined his aunt in prayer for their safety was.

Claire, praying? She'd probably just been polite. He'd like to know for sure, but it was hardly likely she'd tell him, even if he brought it up.

Fresh asparagus, green and tender, poked from wicker baskets, and strawberries glistened red and shiny. Leaf lettuce and green onions vied for space, and a small crowd had gathered in front of a stand that advertised Eastern Shore melons.

There'd been a farmers' market on this block in the oldest part of Suffolk for more than a couple of centuries. Those early residents hadn't gotten melons from the Maryland shore back in the 1700s.

He walked through the wide open doors of the hundred-year-old brick building that housed the more permanent stalls, his mind still occupied with Claire. He'd like to claim his interest was purely spiritual, but he couldn't lie to himself. He was interested in more than Claire's soul, and he didn't quite know what to do with that fact.

He rounded a corner in front of the Amish butcher's counter and stopped. Claire stood a few feet away, juggling a Philly cheesesteak and a soda.

Well, why not? Fully a quarter of the people who jammed the aisles were probably office workers from nearby buildings, and Gray Enterprises wasn't more than a block away. He moved next to her.

"That thing will clog your arteries, you know that, don't you?"

Claire turned toward him and blinked. "What are you doing here?"

"Everyone comes to the farmers' market." He rescued the napkin that was slipping between her fingers. "I'm in search of raspberries for one of my parishioners." He nodded to the sandwich. "You're taking your health in your hands for lunch, obviously."

She looked nettled. "I only indulge in these things once a month or so, not that my health is your concern."

"I understand mine was yours last night, from what Aunt Siobhan says."

Claire's full lips tightened, and she made a business of wrapping her sandwich, but she didn't pretend not to know what he was talking about. "She asked me to pray with her. I could hardly refuse."

"God must have been listening. No one was hurt."

"Do you honestly think that's why?" Her words should have sounded sarcastic, but he caught a serious undertone, as if she really wanted an answer.

"I wouldn't be blaming God today if someone had been hurt," he said carefully. "That's the risk of living in this world instead of the next. But I do believe prayer is important. So thanks for your prayers, whether you meant them or not."

They'd moved so quickly from casual to soul depth. How was it that they'd formed this close a bond in such a short period of time? Especially since they seemed to be disagreeing in most of their conversations.

"I don't—" She stopped, seeming to reconsider what she'd been about to say. "Well, I'm glad everyone is safe. I think your aunt appreciated having Stacy there for company while everyone was at the fire."

"And you."

She shrugged. "I left."

*Not until after you knew we were all okay. Why is it so hard to admit that?*

Something told him to leave it alone for now. There was another subject he needed to discuss with her, anyway.

"Stacy mentioned that you were going with her to Ted's apartment today to collect some of her things."

She nodded, obviously relieved at the change of subject. "I'll pick her up at your aunt's around four. That's the earliest I can get away from the office, but she says Ted will be at work then, so we can get in and out with him none the wiser."

He could only hope Stacy was right about that. Steady employment had never been Ted's strong suit.

"Let me go with you, all right? I don't want the two of you going alone."

She didn't like the suggestion that she couldn't take care of herself—he saw that in her eyes.

"We won't be alone. We'll be together."

He gave in to the impulse to clasp her wrist, feeling smooth skin and a pulse that thudded against his fingers. He also felt her resistance. "Please. Humor me. It's not such a big deal to stop at the church for me, is it?"

"I—"

"Hello, Claire. Having lunch with a friend, are you?"

The voice that interrupted them belonged to a man who might have been one of a dozen businessmen lined up to buy sandwiches. Tall, well-dressed, eyeing them curiously over the steam from his coffee.

"Just getting something to take back to the office." Claire took a step away from Brendan, the gesture implying that they weren't together.

"Jeff Phillips."

The man held out his hand, forcing Brendan to take it. Claire was looking daggers at him for some reason, but he couldn't ignore the gesture.

"Brendan Flanagan." He shook hands briefly.

"Are you—"

"I think they're calling your order." Claire interrupted the man before he could get the question out. "Excuse me. I have to get back to the office."

She spun and moved quickly down the aisle without a backward glance, her departure just short of outright rudeness.

She'd obviously prefer that Brendan head in the opposite direction, but he wasn't going to do that. Instead he followed her, curious. She went out the door onto the street, and he waited until the crowd had closed behind them before he fell into step with her and spoke.

"Friend of yours?"

She shot him an annoyed look, as if asking why he was still there. "Friend? Hardly. A 'colleague' who would stab me in the back if he thought it would do his career any good."

"He seemed friendly enough."

"Believe me, Jeff doesn't know the meaning of the word. He wants my job, and he'd do anything to get it."

He processed that, adding it up to the obvious conclusion. "You don't like it that he saw us together. You think he'll say something to Gray."

"He shouldn't realize that there's anything to tell, but you'd be amazed at how little escapes that man. I have to be on guard every moment."

She was actually serious.

"You make it sound like your job is in some sort of a war zone."

"It is. They don't call it the rat race for nothing."

"That's not a very comfortable way to live, is it?"

Her lips tightened, and for a brief, insane moment he wondered what she'd do if he dropped a kiss on those lips. Slap him, probably.

Not that he would. He had enough trouble with the woman without adding that. He shouldn't even be thinking it, but somehow Claire had flipped his usual control upside down.

"That's my life." Her tone was uncompromising. "And if you'll excuse me, I have to get back to it."

"Right." He rejected the impulse to continue walking along beside her. "Just remember what I said about going to Ted's, okay? Stop by the church for me on your way."

For a moment he thought she'd refuse, but then she shrugged. "I don't think it's necessary, but if it matters that much to you, we'll pick you up."

"It matters," he said. But she'd already swung around and started off down the street, and she gave no sign that she'd heard him.


"Are you mad at the Rev?"

Stacy fiddled with a strand of her long hair as she asked the question, and Claire had to suppress the urge to tell her to leave her hair alone. She wasn't Stacy's mother, after all. She was only—what? A friend? An advisor? A reluctant ally? She wasn't sure just what her role was.

"I'm not mad at him."

Claire frowned at the late afternoon traffic that clogged the narrow street leading away from the church. This part of Suffolk, with its gracious brick houses and tree-lined streets, had an old-world charm, but it could be miserable to get through at rush hour.

She glanced at her watch. They didn't have all that much time, and they'd already wasted some of it waiting at the church for Brendan.

"You act like you are." Stacy was persistent.

"Well, I'm not." But he was the one who'd insisted they stop at the church for him, the one who'd made such a big deal out of their not going alone to Ted's apartment. "He slowed us down, that's all."

"The Rev couldn't help it if somebody else needed him."

Stacy was being a lot nicer than she was about Brendan's defection. He'd said he'd go with them, and instead there'd been a message from him, saying he was detained and to please wait.

But they couldn't wait, because she had no intention of walking right into Ted while trying to collect Stacy's things. An unpleasant shiver snaked down her back at the thought, and she dismissed it angrily.

Let that be a lesson to you, she lectured herself. You can't count on people, even those with the best intentions.

She'd counted on Bruce when she'd stood with him in front of a justice of the peace and believed the promises he'd made. She'd learned the truth the hard way. It was better to control your own destiny.

"Maybe we should have waited for him." Stacy looked out the car window, and Claire could feel the tension rising as they neared the block where Ted's apartment was.

"Not unless we wanted to risk running into Ted." She started looking for a parking place in the crowded block of elderly apartment buildings. "Look, we'll get in and out in a hurry. It'll be fine."

Was Stacy worried about what Ted would do if he found them, or worried about how she'd act if he did show up? She could understand that, only too well.

"There's a place, right in front." Stacy's hands twisted together, but she sounded determined.

Well, good. The kid had a right to collect her own belongings without being afraid.

Claire parked, then got out and locked the car. Even in the daytime, she didn't like leaving the car on the street here, but it couldn't be helped. This had probably once been a decent neighborhood, but not any longer.

She stepped over the trash in the gutter and followed Stacy into the dim hallway.

"The apartment is on the second floor." Stacy started up a flight of dusty stairs.

Claire tried not to inhale, preferring not to identify the smells. "You have a key?"

She found she was keeping her voice low. Not that she was afraid, but there was no point in advertising their presence.

Stacy nodded, stopping in front of a battered door.

She seemed to steel herself. Then she unlocked the door, pushed it open and stepped through.

Claire followed her, muscles tight. As soon as the door closed behind them, relief swept over her. Clearly they were alone. The whole apartment consisted of one messy room with no place for any human sized creature to hide. Jeans and T-shirts were strewn on the floor, and pizza crusts littered the table in the kitchen area.

"Ted's kind of messy." Stacy took a step toward the kitchen, as if intending to clean it up.

Claire caught her arm. "Never mind that. If Ted wants to live like a pig, that's his problem. Let's just get your clothes."

Stacy nodded, then took the duffel bag Claire held out to her. "It'll just take a couple minutes. I don't have much stuff here."

The poor kid didn't have much stuff anywhere, as far as Claire could tell. One thing they'd do before Stacy had another job interview was go shopping. At least she could afford to give the girl a decent interview outfit. And maybe a haircut, too, if Stacy would agree.

Stacy jerked open a dresser drawer and began shoving clothes into the duffel bag haphazardly. Her tension was both palpable and contagious. Claire found herself glancing toward the door.

She'd done this before. Scurried around a tiny apartment, trying to clean up, hoping there was nothing that would set Bruce off. At the time, she'd probably known inside that nothing she did would make a difference, but she'd done it anyway. That was a trap abused women fell into so easily, thinking they were to blame for what happened.

If the abuser's temper exploded out of control, that was his problem, not yours. She'd learned that, eventually. Too late. If she could help it, Stacy wasn't going to learn things the hard way.

She glanced at Stacy, who stood irresolute, an iron in her hand.

"What's wrong?"

"I don't know whether to take this or not. I bought it at the thrift shop, but Ted doesn't have one. If he wants to iron something—"

"Since Ted seems to store most of his clothes on the floor, I'd guess he doesn't have much use for an iron, does he?"

Stacy managed a weak grin. "Guess not."

"Take it. Is that everything?"

"I think so." Stacy stuffed it in the bag, glancing around. "I—"

Whatever else she'd intended to say was lost in the rattle of a key in the lock. She froze. The apartment door swung open, and Ted stood there, seeming to fill the doorway.

"You came back."

For an instant a smile lightened his sulky face, and Claire glimpsed the charm that had probably attracted Stacy to begin with. Then he seemed to register the bag she held, and his face closed down.

"What are you doing?" He ground out the words, taking a step toward the girl.

Stacy made some indeterminate sound, and Claire's stomach turned over as she recognized the symptoms. Stacy was too scared to speak. Any hope that she'd stand up for herself vanished.

Claire forced herself to move between them. "Stacy is getting some of her things." She kept her voice neutral. If they could just keep this from spiraling out of control, they could get out.

A heavy frown settled on Ted's face as he focused on her. "I know who you are. You're the one who's been telling Stacy I'm no good for her."

"You told Stacy that when you hit her. She didn't need anyone else to explain it to her." It was amazing that her voice could sound so calm when her stomach was busy tying itself in knots.

Ted's fists bunched, the muscles standing out on his arms.

Anger mixed with fear flooded through her. You said you'd come with me, Brendan. You let me down.

Ted looked past her at Stacy. "Come on, baby. You don't want to go. We were happy, weren't we?" His voice lowered, coaxing. "You remember the good times, Stace. Don't you?"

"Yes." Stacy's voice was a whisper. "I remember."

"Come back to me, baby. It'll be good again, I promise."

How many times had she heard that, believed that,

gone back? A flicker of pain went through her, sharp and distinct from the anger and the fear. She'd lost her baby because she'd believed those promises.

She swung toward Stacy, seeing the weakening in the girl's expression. Her anger took over, sharp and bracing.

"Stacy, don't be an idiot. How long have his promises lasted before? A day or two? Then something makes him mad and he takes it out on you. It won't be any different this time."

"You stay out of this." The fury in Ted's voice reverberated in her head, bringing back echoes from the past. "It's none of your business."

"I care about Stacy. That makes it my business."

Anger distorted Ted's features, and for an instant it might have been Bruce looking at her, Bruce swearing at her.

"Get out!" Ted lifted a heavy fist. "Get out and leave us alone."

For a terrible instant the fear almost made her cower away from him. She tried to beat it back. She couldn't let it take control again. But even as she thought that, she felt herself weakening—felt the fear rising, taking over.

He must sense that, because he took a step toward her, as if he'd sweep her out of his way.

*Help me.* The words formed in her mind without a conscious decision. *Help us. If You're as real as Brendan thinks You are, help us.*

Ridiculous. She didn't believe. How could she cry out to Someone she didn't believe in?

Ridiculous or not, she suddenly seemed to see the situation clearly. She wasn't a helpless teenager with nowhere to go. She was a grown woman, a successful businesswoman. She wasn't about to let some punk push her around.

"We're leaving." The words were suffused with enough power to make Ted pause. "We're taking Stacy's things and going, so just get out of our way unless you want to get more trouble than you know what to do with."

"Yeah? Who's gonna give me trouble? You?"

"Stacy has friends now." Amazing, the confidence that flooded her, washing away any trace of fear. "We won't let her be hurt again. So just back off."

Hesitation flickered in his eyes at her words, and she knew he was weakening.

"Come on, Stacy." She grabbed the girl's arm. "We're done here."

She shoved Stacy toward the door, watching as Ted fell back a step. It seemed she held that confidence as a shield, protecting them from any harm.

Her muscles tensed as they reached the point where she had to turn her back on Ted to open the door, but he didn't move. She pushed Stacy out into the hallway and slammed the door behind them.

"Hurry." Stacy's face had lost all its color, but she grabbed the rail and started down.

Claire followed her, senses alert for any hint that Ted was coming after them. Nothing.

They made it down the dingy stairs and out into the late afternoon sunlight.

"We're safe." She clutched Stacy's arm. "It's okay." She almost felt like laughing. They *were* safe.

Stacy gave a shaky laugh that sounded as if it could spill over into hysteria at any moment. "You were so awesome. You were so brave."

Brave? The word echoed in her mind as they got into the car and she pulled back into traffic.

She'd had the courage inside her. She'd just needed to remind herself of who she was, even if she'd had that momentary impulse to cry out to God. She'd been around Brendan and his church people a little too much lately. He could believe in answered prayers all he wanted. She didn't.

## Chapter Eight

Claire didn't realize that her legs were trembling until after she'd dropped Stacy off and arrived at her town house. It hit her when she got out of the car. She stood for a moment, hand on the car door, letting herself adjust.

Okay, deal with it. She was going to be all right, if sandbagged by the aftermath of such an emotional encounter.

This had been the sort of encounter she'd spent the past ten years avoiding, until Brendan got her involved with Stacy. She added that to the number of reasons she had to be angry with Brendan right now.

The fact that he stood waiting on her front step didn't help matters any.

"Claire, thank heavens." Brendan hurried to meet her on the sidewalk, grasping her arms as if checking for bruises. "Are you all right?"

Anger surged through her. How could he ask that,

after the way he'd let her down? She jerked her arms free, giving him the full blast of her anger.

"I'm fine. So is Stacy. No thanks to you. What are you doing here, anyway?"

And why don't you go away? She didn't want to deal with him, not now. Maybe later, when she had herself back under control again.

She stalked past him and thrust her key in the lock. All she wanted was to get into her own private sanctuary and regroup. Surely he would leave now.

But he stayed at her heels, leaning against the door frame as she struggled with the lock.

"My secretary told me you and Stacy had left. I've been all over town trying to find you. I went to Ted's, but no one was there."

He must have just missed them. Well, that was fine. They'd managed on their own, hadn't they? She pushed away thoughts of that surge of confidence that had seemed to come out of nowhere.

"Finally, Aunt Siobhan called and told me you'd dropped Stacy off and you were on your way home. I had to be sure you're all right."

"Well, now you see that I am." She pushed the door open and stepped into the stillness of her own place.

"Are you sure you're okay? Ted didn't touch either of you?"

Brendan pushed into the hallway after her. Clearly he had no intention of leaving until he was assured she was safe. Guilt, probably, because he hadn't been there.

Well, she didn't want his disturbing presence in her private sanctuary. She dropped her keys into the basket on the hall table. She'd bought the table in an unfinished furniture shop, liking its clean, simple lines, and then painted it a pale cream color to match the walls. It was part of the ordered world she'd created. That orderliness was what she needed right now.

But she couldn't relax until she'd gotten rid of Brendan. She swung to face him, wondering where all her confidence had gone. She felt like collapsing on the couch and pulling a blanket over her head.

"I said I'm fine."

He shook his head, as if trying to shake off a bad dream. "You and Stacy shouldn't have gone without me. What were you thinking?"

"What was I thinking?" Her control slipped, her anger bubbling up. "You're the one who didn't show up when you were supposed to. You let me down. Let us down," she corrected quickly.

This wasn't about her and Brendan. There was no her and Brendan.

"I left a message for you." His dark brows drew down over his eyes. "One of my parishioners had an emergency. I got back to the church as soon as I could, and you were gone. Why didn't you wait?"

Of course he had an excuse. People always did when they let you down.

"We couldn't. Stacy was afraid Ted would come home from work if we delayed going any longer."

She turned away, the energy provided by her anger seeping away. Brendan hadn't been there for them because someone else needed him. That was how it would be for anyone foolish enough to get involved with someone like Brendan—always taking a back seat to other people's needs.

"Ted came anyway, didn't he? When I think what could have happened—" He broke off, shaking his head. Then he took her arm. "I'm sorry. I shouldn't keep you standing here. Come and sit down."

He led her into the living room as if it were his own, guiding her to the leather couch. She ought to tell him to go away, but she couldn't seem to muster up the strength.

She sank onto the couch, welcoming its familiar comfort. Then Brendan sat down next to her, his presence disturbing the equilibrium. His hand covered hers warmly. "How did Stacy take it?"

Against her will, a shudder went through her. "Not well. If I hadn't been with her, I'm afraid she'd have gone back to him."

The shudder seemed to continue deep inside her, like the aftershocks from an earthquake. She knew, too well, what the result of that would have been.

She felt his fingers tighten on hers. Almost without thinking it, she turned her hand so that they were palm to palm. A wave of warmth generated by that touch seemed to travel up her arm.

"You were there." His voice was tight, almost as if with anger. "You didn't let that happen to her."

She met his gaze, searching for what he was feeling. "What is it, Brendan? Does that make you angry?"

Even as she said the words, she realized something strange. She'd never seen Brendan angry. Annoyed, yes. She managed to annoy him on a regular basis. But angry? Never.

"It's not anger." His voice deepened, and his fingers interlaced with hers, the touch astonishingly intimate. "It's caring. I care about you. You know that, don't you?"

She couldn't find her voice. The annoyance she so often felt with him vanished in the piercing strength of his gaze. Her heart began to beat in slow, deafening thuds.

Brendan's eyes darkened as he searched her face. She heard the deep intake of his breath, and then he stroked her cheek with a feather-light touch. His hand set up impulses that raced along her skin.

"Brendan—"

His hand slid into her hair, and his lips found hers.

Rational thought vanished. She couldn't think, only feel—warmth, tenderness, longing. She wanted the moment to last, wanted his arms close around her and his lips on hers. All the cold, sharp things in her world were vanquished by his touch.

"Claire." He said her name softly against her lips, and then he put his cheek against hers. She felt a chuckle deep in his chest under her hand. "I didn't know that was going to happen. Should I apologize?"

"Not unless you regret it."

She drew back a little, so that she could see his eyes.

She was on unfamiliar territory now. There hadn't been anyone in her life for a very long time. She hadn't thought she needed anyone. Maybe she still didn't, but Brendan had made her wonder.

"No. No regrets." He cupped her cheek with his hand. "I'm just so relieved you're safe I couldn't help myself."

She managed a shaky laugh. "Is this the treatment for anxiety they teach in seminary?"

He clasped her hand in both of his, leaning back against the couch and watching her. There was a steady glow in his eyes that made them look a deep green. She hadn't seen that look before.

"Not likely. This only happens with you. I was relieved to know that Stacy was safe, but I wasn't moved to kiss her."

She leaned back next to him, their shoulders touching. The shakiness was gone, replaced by a profound sense of well-being. "I'm glad. That would certainly complicate matters."

The faintest frown touched his brow. "Poor Stacy. If what you say is true—" He hesitated, then shook his head. "What could possibly make her even think about going back to Ted after what he's done? I could understand her having trouble getting out in the first place, but not going back."

"It's not so unusual." She took a deep breath, knowing suddenly that she was going to tell him.

For a moment all her barriers went up. She didn't tell people. But Brendan wasn't just people. He'd come too far into her life to pretend otherwise. And she couldn't let him get this close to her without being honest.

"Claire?" He looked puzzled. "What is it?"

"I can understand why Stacy almost went back," she said evenly. "I can understand, because I did the same thing."

For a moment there was blank incomprehension in his eyes. Then she saw the realization dawn.

"If you pity me, I'll hit you," she warned.

"Not pity. Caring. Remember?"

She nodded. It was all right. Brendan was safe. She now knew he was one of the few people in this world she could tell her story to and know that it wouldn't make him look down on her. Or cause him to use it against her.

"How old were you?"

She could see that he was feeling his way, not sure what to ask.

"Eighteen. Two years older than Stacy, but still not old enough."

"Your family?"

She couldn't just tell him part of it. The honest way was to tell him the whole story.

"I told you that my mother died when I was young— just nine."

"That was terrible." The deep note in Brendan's voice told her he understood. He'd lost his mother, too.

She nodded. "I guess I was luckier than you were. I still had my dad, and we were very close." She knew the smile that touched her lips was bittersweet. "I remember how proud I was when he came to the school for parent nights and concerts and plays. He never missed one single thing. I could always look out into the audience and see him there."

"But then something changed. What was it?"

His intuitiveness must make him a good minister. She nodded.

"He met someone and fell in love. I guess I should have seen it coming, but I didn't. I was a junior in high school when they married."

"The wicked stepmother?"

She frowned, trying to be honest. "That's how I saw her then. Looking back, I suppose she was just trying to establish her relationship with her new husband. But my dad—" She couldn't help the bitterness that crept into her voice. "He was like a kid, head over heels in love. All the attention I was used to having went to her."

"So you looked for attention somewhere else."

A momentary anger flared. "You don't have to be so right all the time, you know."

"I'm sorry." His fingers caressed the back of her hand. "It's what anyone would do who felt she'd lost the most important person in her life."

"Maybe so." She shrugged. "I started going out with Bruce. He was different from the usual acceptable boys I'd dated—edgier." She tried to look rationally at the person she'd been so many years ago. "Maybe I thought that would make my father pay attention. But his wife got pregnant. It was like he didn't even see me anymore."

"The boyfriend—"

"Bruce Sanders." She wasn't proud of what she'd done, but if she was going to tell him, she had to be honest.

"We ran away the night of graduation and got married in front of a justice of the peace." She shook her head. "Stupid. I knew it was wrong even when I was doing it. We hadn't been married more than a few weeks when he started knocking me around."

She could feel Brendan's pain for her through the grip of his hands. Suddenly she didn't want him to be touching her when she told him the rest of it. She got up, walked across the room to the window and stared out, not even attempting to focus on the scene beyond the glass.

She heard him rise, but he seemed to understand that she needed him to keep his distance at this moment.

"You didn't feel you could go to your father with what was happening?"

"We'd had a dramatic four-way scene when Bruce and I got back to town. It was one of those times when everyone says more than they should. My father said if I wanted to be married I shouldn't come back to him for anything." She shook her head, trying to dislodge the memory. "I don't know if he meant it or not, but he never made another effort to stay in touch with me." She rubbed her arms, suddenly cold. "Even now, I can't understand that."

"No. I can't understand it, either. But you eventually got out on your own." Brendan's voice was closer, but he didn't touch her.

"It cost me too much." Her throat closed, and tears stung her eyes. She had to force the words out. "I found out I was pregnant. Like a fool, I thought that would make things better."

Brendan's hands closed over her shoulders, as if to absorb some of the pain.

"He knocked me down the stairs one night. I lost the baby." A tiny cry seemed to pierce her soul, and the sobs she'd held back for so long choked her.

Brendan murmured something inarticulate, and then he turned her around and pulled her against him, his arms holding her tightly.

She fought the tears, but a few spilled over anyway, wetting Brendan's shirt.

"You should have told me when I asked you to help Stacy." His voice was soft against her hair. "I'd never have gotten you involved with her if I'd known."

Much as she longed for the feeling of his arms around her, she didn't want a relationship that was based on pity. She drew back, still in the circle of his arms, and brushed the tears away.

"I didn't know you well enough then to tell you. And maybe it's worked out for the best." Her smile twisted. "Nobody else would understand as well as I do what Stacy is feeling."

He studied her face. "Nobody else would hurt as much, either. It's not fair to you."

"That's what I've been telling myself, but I think it's been good for me, too. I've been so obsessed with my job these last few years that I haven't made time for anything or anyone else. Then Nolie needed my help with the wedding, and you pushed me into helping Stacy." She realized the truth of what she was saying even as she verbalized it. "I found out there was a whole world out there. Professional success isn't enough. I want a life, too."

She looked into Brendan's face, confident that she'd see encouragement and understanding there. After all, he'd kissed her. He'd said he cared.

Instead she saw—nothing. It was as if some sort of curtain had come down between them, and the man who'd held her in his arms had vanished behind it.

The reality of Claire's words sank in to Brendan's heart. She was saying she wanted a relationship. That she was ready to open herself up to the possibility, at least.

He'd kissed her. He'd told her he cared for her.

But he was the last man in the world who could take the risk of a relationship with a woman like Claire.

His thoughts swung dizzily from one thing to another. How could he possibly tell her?

She opened her heart to you. The voice of his conscience sounded remarkably like that of his Aunt Siobhan. You can't hurt her.

I can't get involved with her.

That held the potential for hurting Claire far more than anything else he might say or do now.

He let his hands drop casually from her shoulders. It felt as if he were letting go of a piece of himself.

"I'm glad." That much was true, at least. "I'd hate to think going through all this had hurt you for nothing."

He forced the words to come out in his minister voice— calm, reassuring, sympathetic. Caring, but not personal.

Claire got the message. It took a moment, but then he saw it in the way she drew back, pulling that armor of chilly sophistication around her again.

"That's true." She rubbed her arms as if cold, and he longed to touch her again. To pull her into his arms and kiss away the pain.

He couldn't. He knew, better than anyone, the black anger that lived inside him. And he knew the results of that anger. He'd seen it often enough in his parents.

*Why haven't You taken it away, Father? I've asked so many times.*

That was the prayer God had never answered. He'd lived with the anger, kept it under iron control, felt it surge inside him with danger.

He shouldn't risk something as serious as marriage with anyone, and certainly not with Claire. She'd already been through enough pain for a lifetime. He couldn't expose her to more.

So he had to be her friend. That was all he could offer her.

Claire turned away, seeming to search for some-thing to say that would ease the situation. Something that would let both of them pretend they hadn't gone to the very edge of a relationship before turning back.

"In any event, Stacy is stuck with me now." She sent him a fleeting glance. "I haven't told her about my ex-perience. No one knows, except Nolie. And now you."

And now him. Claire had told him something she didn't tell anyone, and he'd pushed her away. The knowledge was a knife in his heart.

"I won't say anything to anyone." That was certainly the least he could do for her. "But don't you think it might help Stacy if she knew you'd been through the same experience she has?"

"I don't know." She crossed her arms, her body lan-guage rejecting the suggestion that she share her story with the girl. "I'll think about it."

He nodded. "I hope—" He stopped. He hoped so many things, both for Stacy and for Claire, but probably most of them were impossible. "I hope Stacy feels stronger about this situation now. Even if she had to rely on your strength, at least she faced Ted and got through it."

"I'd be happier if Ted disappeared entirely. He could start life again in Miami or Los Angeles or the moon, as far as I'm concerned."

That was probably what she'd hoped about Bruce, as well.

"At least they aren't married," he said.

"That's good. I wish I'd been that fortunate. It took a divorce I couldn't afford to get me out." She darted him a defiant look. "I suppose you think that's wrong."

He met her look steadily. "You're still making assumptions about what I believe based on the collar I wear."

She shrugged. "Maybe I am."

"I don't think divorce should be taken lightly." His heart was in the words. "But sometimes it would be a greater wrong to continue a marriage that's hurting everyone involved. God does allow for mistakes." He managed a smile. "That's a good thing, since His children make so many of them."

If his parents had ended their marriage, they might still be alive. The thought burned its way into his brain.

She sent him a glance he couldn't read. "I used to believe church people thought they were perfect and the rest of us were hopelessly wrong."

"Used to?"

"Well, since I've gotten to know you—"

He found he was smiling. A few minutes ago he wouldn't have believed he and Claire could ever share a smile with each other again.

"Since you met me, now you know just how nonperfect we are. Well, I'm glad I've exposed you to that truth, at least, even if I never wanted to be such a terrible example."

"Not terrible. Just human."

Claire's smile was more natural and relaxed, too. Maybe they would eventually be able to move back to the friendship they'd begun before he'd made the mistake of getting too close.

But he wouldn't forget, not easily. He and Claire might be able to be friends, at least. But he'd never forget that they could have been much more to each other, if not for the darkness that lived inside him.

# Chapter Nine

"Are you sure about this?" Stacy clutched the hairdresser's cape with both hands and stared at Claire's reflection in the mirror. "It took a long time to grow my hair this long." Her hair, fresh from shampooing, hung straight and lank to below her shoulders.

"Trust me." Claire exchanged a glance with Mona Phillips, who'd been her hairdresser since she'd come to Suffolk. "Mona will make you look like a person anyone would want to hire. You want that job, don't you?"

Maybe stocking merchandise at Gray's Department Store didn't sound like a big deal, but Stacy was thrilled with the opportunity Claire had arranged.

"I sure do." Her clutch eased, and she took a deep breath. "Okay. Do it."

Mona gave the girl a reassuring smile as she twisted a length of hair to the top of Stacy's head and pinned it there. "Just relax. I won't make it too short, and besides, hair will always grow back if you don't like the style."

Stacy nodded, and Claire leaned back in her chair. This experiment was going to work. They'd already shopped for clothes, and Stacy was ecstatic about the new skirt, pants and lightweight sweaters she now owned. Once she saw her new image, she'd never want to go back.

"I was thinking." Stacy closed her eyes, as if reluctant to watch as hair started to fall to the floor. "Maybe, if I get a good enough job, I'd be able to take care of the baby by myself."

Claire bit back the impulse to tell Stacy exactly what she thought of that idea. As Brendan had said, Stacy needed advice, but she was the one who had to live with the results of her decisions.

"I'm sure you're going to get a good summer job," she said carefully. "But I think you ought to consider finishing high school. It's really tough to find a good permanent job without a high school diploma."

"My friend Jody didn't graduate high school. She's a waitress, and she makes lots in tips."

She hoped she looked as if she were considering that. "Is Jody supporting a baby?"

"Well, no." Stacy frowned. "The Rev thinks I ought to get my diploma, too. He's usually right about stuff, don't you think?"

"Yes, he usually is." She kept her voice even with an effort. Had Brendan been right when he'd kissed her and then backed away?

Well, maybe he *had* been right, at that. If he didn't want a relationship with her, it was just as well to know that before they became involved any more deeply in each other's lives.

And he didn't. His response had made that clear.

Had he backed off because of what she'd revealed to him about her past? She'd never know the answer to that one.

She didn't want a serious relationship, either, so that was fine. She'd been carried away by the emotion of the moment, and maybe he had been, too. She'd decided a long time ago that she wouldn't risk getting serious about anyone, and there was no good reason to change her mind just because weddings were in the air.

She wrestled with the situation while Mona clipped her way through Stacy's locks. Was that all it was? The fact that most of her mind was given over to Nolie's wedding, combined with the sheer joy she witnessed every time she saw Nolie and Gabe together?

Then there was the added fact that Brendan was too appealing for his own good. The only surprising thing was that one of his single parishioners hadn't shanghaied him to the altar before now.

"If I gave the baby up for adoption—" Stacy stopped and swallowed hard. Her thoughts had obviously been even more troubling than Claire's. "If I do, how will I know that he's going to get a really good home?"

Stacy was asking for advice on the most serious decision she'd probably ever make in her life. For a moment Claire felt a surge of panic. Who was she to give advice on a subject like this? She'd made more mistakes for sorrier reasons than Stacy ever had.

She had to try. She'd committed herself to helping the girl, and that meant she had to do the best she could, no matter how unqualified she felt.

"I don't suppose there are any guarantees," she said carefully. "But I know that the agency your social worker recommended has a great reputation. You'd know that the baby was going to have two parents who really long for a child and can't have one of their own. I expect that means they've got a lot of love to give."

Stacy didn't give any sign that she agreed or disagreed. Instead, she fixed her gaze on a display of hairspray at the end of the counter.

"My mother never really wanted to have a baby." Her shoulders moved under the plastic cape. "Neither did my dad, I guess."

It was tough to keep her voice even when her heart was breaking for the girl. "You can give your baby two parents who really want him."

Two big tears welled up in Stacy's eyes, but she blinked them back. "Maybe," she said softly.

She'd have to be content with that. She couldn't push Stacy into a decision she wasn't ready to make.

Mona ruffled Stacy's hair with a gentle hand, then started the hairdryer. The noise cut off any further conversation. Maybe that was just as well. She and Stacy had given each other enough to think about for the moment.

For just an instant, a flare of resentment at Brendan flickered through her heart. If he hadn't gotten her involved in this situation with Stacy, she wouldn't have anything more serious to worry about right now than the menu for the wedding reception.

Then who would be helping Stacy? Probably Brendan would say that her involvement with the girl was meant to be. That somehow God had planned all that.

She didn't buy that idea. Of course she didn't.

Still, she was involved, and she'd do her best by the girl. She'd help her get a decent summer job and try to build up her confidence so that Stacy wouldn't dream of letting anyone hurt her again.

And while she was making all these fine resolutions, she'd better make it clear to Brendan that all she wanted or expected from him was friendship.

Now if she could just convince herself of that fact, she'd be able to concentrate on the wedding without any stray daydreams making her think she wanted something that was clearly out of the question.

Brendan followed Gabe and Nolie up the walk of Claire's town house that evening, slowing down as he approached the steps. He couldn't be there without remembering how he'd felt waiting for Claire to return from that insane encounter with Ted.

"Are you sure it was all right with Claire for me to come this evening?" He'd think she'd be just as happy if she never had to look at him again.

Nolie glanced over her shoulder at him. "Of course. This is the only evening we have free this week, so we may as well make as many decisions as we can about both the wedding and the reception. Claire understands that."

Would Claire have told Nolie about what had happened between them? They seemed to share just about everything, so she probably had.

If so, Nolie didn't seem to be holding it against him. Her smile, when she and Gabe had met him at the Flanagan house, had been as warm as ever.

Maybe Nolie was imagining a happy ending for her best friend and Gabe's cousin. He hoped not, because she'd be in for a disappointment.

No happy endings for you, he reminded himself. At least not romantic ones. He'd better keep that in mind, because otherwise someone could get hurt.

He was still telling himself that when Claire opened the door, and he discovered that he became short of breath just looking at her.

In the general hubbub of greetings he was able to get himself under strict control, so that by the time Claire finished hugging Nolie and Gabe, he had a smile and a handshake ready.

If she thought the handshake odd, she didn't betray that. Her smile seemed a little fixed, but her voice sounded perfectly normal.

"Please, come in. I understand we're going to whip through dozens of decisions tonight."

"So they tell me." He hoped he sounded as cool and

collected as she did. He would not glance toward the spot where they'd been when he kissed her.

"Mom would have been happy to have you come over for supper tonight, you know." Gabe made a hand sign to Max, and the yellow Labrador flopped down on the rug next to the sofa.

"She's doing too much already." Claire lifted the coffeepot from the service she had ready on the table. "I thought we could probably get through this without any additional calories, so I just fixed coffee."

"Coffee's fine. Maybe it'll keep us awake." Nolie sat down next to Gabe. "You wouldn't believe the paperwork that's been keeping us up at nights."

Brendan took the leather easy chair that sat at a right angle to the sofa. That would put Claire opposite him, but that was better than sitting next to her. Look what had happened the last time he'd done that.

"That's how it is when you get involved with a foundation that hands out money," he said.

"You just wish they'd send some your way for your teenagers," Gabe retorted.

"It wouldn't hurt. The shoestring I'm operating on has gotten pretty frayed."

"If Stacy's an example of the good work you're doing, it's well worth it." Nolie's smile included him and Claire both. "She gave us a fashion show of her new job-interview clothes and her haircut. She looks fantastic. You wouldn't know she was the same girl."

"That's all Claire's doing," he said quickly, holding

up his hands to push away any part of it. "I can't claim any credit for that."

"It was your idea," Claire said. He couldn't be sure whether that was an edge to her voice or not. She surely wasn't still annoyed with him for getting her involved with Stacy, was she? "All I did was add the professional expertise. I know how to help her get a job."

His gaze met Claire's across the coffee table, and he suddenly felt as if they were alone in the room again. "She has you worried about everything other than the job, doesn't she?"

A spasm of pain crossed her face. "She was talking today about the decision to give up the baby."

She was hurting, and he didn't have the right to comfort her. He'd given that up.

"Poor girl." Nolie's voice was soft. "She must really be struggling with that."

And every moment she struggled just reminded Claire of her own loss. The guilt he felt for involving her in the situation was a weight on his soul.

"Well, that's not why we're here." Claire seemed to shake off the pain, but probably everyone in the room knew she couldn't. "We've got a wedding and reception to plan, remember?"

In the face of Claire's determination, they couldn't do anything but go along with the pretense that she was all right and that Stacy's pain hadn't multiplied her own.

But she wasn't all right, and he knew it. They seemed

to be speaking to each other without the need for words or touch, as if heart spoke to heart, soul to soul.

He would not let this be love. Because that way lay disaster for both of them.

Two hours later they'd hammered out every decision that had yet to be made about the wedding, and Brendan could only wonder if everyone else felt as exhausted as he did. He'd never have imagined there were so many decisions to make. He'd always just come in at the part labeled "Officiant," and the rest of the work had been done by someone else.

Gabe leaned back against the sofa, obviously relieved that he'd finally convinced Claire to allow the Flanagan family to bear their share of the reception cost. Nolie, nestled next to him, glowed with pleasure that her two families were united in the celebration of their wedding.

Claire had the look that she probably wore when she'd closed a big business deal. It had been a tough negotiation, and she'd had to give a bit, but for the most part she'd gotten what she wanted.

Was he the only one sitting here feeling as if there were a hole in his heart? Apparently so.

Claire picked up the coffee tray, obviously headed for the kitchen. It wasn't safe to be alone with her, but he didn't have a choice. He had to follow her. Somehow he had to let her know….

What? He couldn't tell her the confusion of feelings

that battered him when he was in her presence. He couldn't let her guess that he felt anything more than friendship. So what did he have to say?

Still, he took the coffeepot and followed her into the kitchen.

"Here's the pot," he said unnecessarily, setting it on the counter. He hadn't been in her kitchen before. He couldn't help but stare. The room was small, very neat, and perfectly white. Even the floor was white.

"Are you disapproving of my kitchen?" She seemed able to read his mind.

"Not at all. I just can't imagine keeping a kitchen looking this pristine. Mine usually looks as if the Civil War had been fought in there, especially when I've been cooking spaghetti."

"Maybe that's why you eat so many meals at your aunt and uncle's house."

"Well, I do that mostly for the company. I hate to eat alone." He didn't seem to be getting very far with saying anything that would help the situation between them.

Probably the most sensible thing to do was avoid Claire entirely until this crazy feeling went away. Unfortunately, the possibility of avoiding her while they were in the midst of putting on the wedding was small, to say nothing of their other involvement.

She began stacking cups in the sink, her back to him. He discovered he was studying the long, slim curve of her back and the way her hair curved toward her cheek in a bronze wave. She lifted her hand to brush her hair back behind her ear, and the desire to brush his lips against her cheek nearly swamped all his good intentions.

She rinsed the coffeepot. "I usually just grab a salad on my way home from work."

It took a moment to remember what they'd been talking about, so that he could make sense of her comment.

"I'd think you'd need more than a salad after a full day of work."

She shrugged, turning to face him. "I'm usually too tired to bother. Anyway, what did you think of Stacy's new look? You haven't said."

*Because I was afraid of bringing up a subject that might hurt you.*

"She looks wonderful, thanks to you. More importantly, she knows she looks good."

"That is important." Her quick glance approved of his insight. She leaned back against the white counter, hands braced against its edge. "If she feels good about herself, more confident, she'll be less likely to let someone treat her badly."

It was hard to imagine Claire looking any way but polished, elegant and professional. Had she fought her way to that look, too?

He couldn't let himself keep thinking this way. He couldn't go on imagining what her life had been, what she was thinking, what she was feeling.

Once this wedding was over, they weren't going to be anything more to each other than casual acquaintances, connected by mutual friends. He might see her occasionally at Gabe and Nolie's, but that would be all.

"I'm grateful for everything you're doing for her." That sounded ridiculously formal, but he didn't know what else to say.

She nodded. "It's going to be all right, I think. She's moving toward a decision to let the baby be adopted. It's hard, but I think she'll do the right thing."

"I've been praying about it. Praying for you, too, every time you meet with her."

Claire probably didn't want to hear that, but he had to say it. Even casual acquaintances could pray for each other, couldn't they?

"Thank you." Her words sounded just as formal as his had been.

They seemed to have covered everything. Stacy was doing better, and Claire sounded increasingly confident about helping her. Most of the wedding decisions had been made, and in a few weeks that would be over.

They were moving on. He still felt as if there was a hole in his heart, but maybe he'd get used to that, in time. Seeing less of Claire would undoubtedly help.

"Gabe and Nolie are probably about ready to go." He turned toward the door, only to be stopped by the touch of her hand on his arm.

He swung back to her. Her hand dropped away instantly, as if she'd touched something hot.

"One more thing." She hesitated as if, whatever it was, she found it difficult to say.

He tried to look receptive, tried not to pray that she wouldn't mention that kiss.

"I don't want what happened the last time you were here to stand between us." Claire's chin firmed, as if she'd decided what she was going to say and was determined to say it, no matter how difficult.

That was Claire, wasn't it? He already knew that about her. She wouldn't take the easy way out.

"It won't." He could be just as courageous about this as she was, even though he knew he was lying through his teeth. The damage had already been done. "You don't need to worry about that. It won't affect how we work together."

"Good." Her smile flickered. "This wedding has to go off without a hitch, or Nolie will never let me forget that I pushed her into it."

"Don't worry about it. I promise, at the end of the day they'll be married. That's the important thing."

And when it happened, his relationship with Claire would be at an end.

"It's not just that, as important as that is." Claire looked up at him, her gaze serious. "I'd never expected to have a minister for a friend, but it seems to have happened. I'd hate to lose that just because we were both overwrought about what happened."

Friends.

What I want from you isn't friendship, Claire. Or at least, that's not all. But it's what I'll have to settle for, because anything closer is out of the question.

He managed a smile. "You don't need to worry. I'm happy to be considered your friend."

And I'll never ask for anything else.

# Chapter Ten

"See?" Nolie smiled at Claire across the dining room table at the Flanagan house. "I told you this would be more fun with everyone helping."

Claire managed to return the smile as she moved a pair of scissors out of reach of an inquisitive four-year-old. They'd been making favors out of squares of netting, and Mary Kate's two youngsters were determined to help.

"I just didn't want to impose." *I wanted to do it myself. Well, she couldn't say that, could she?*

Siobhan smacked Brendan's hand lightly as he reached over her shoulder in an attempt to steal a handful of candy-coated almonds. "Some of us are being more helpful than others," she commented.

"Hey, I'm working." He sounded playfully wounded, almost lighthearted, as if when he walked through the front door of the Flanagan house, the burden of his pastoral duties fell away and he could be a kid again. "I hung the crepe paper, didn't I?"

"You?" Ryan leaned on the back of his sister's chair, his blue eyes mocking. "You wouldn't know a day's work if it stared you in the face."

Brendan tossed a piece of confetti at his cousin. "A lot you know about it, sitting around the firehouse eating chili. Claire, tell my aunt I deserve a handful of candy for helping."

Appealed to, she had to try and join in, but she wasn't used to the casual kidding the Flanagans inflicted on each other as naturally as breathing.

"I did see him put up one decoration," she said. "I'm not sure how much candy that merits."

"None," Siobhan said, but then gave him a handful, laughing. "You boys never grow up, do you? You're still eating us out of house and home."

Ryan snatched up a handful of candy and blew a kiss to his mother. "If you run out, I'll go buy some more. I'll charge it to Brendan."

"What makes you think I have any money?" Brendan cuffed him lightly. "Come on, let's hang the rest of these decorations before they really do cut us off. Terry, come tell us where the wedding bells go."

He went back into the living room, and she could breathe naturally again. Not that being this close to Brendan bothered her, she assured herself. Why would it? They were friends, and that was all. They'd settled that between them several nights ago. Just because they were spending a Saturday afternoon together getting ready for the shower didn't mean she had to overreact.

And just because he'd shown up wearing shorts and a Suffolk Fire Department T-shirt that showed off every muscle didn't mean she had to notice, did it?

Friends, she reminded herself. She frowned at the strip of ribbon she'd been trying to tie around the favor. It looked as if she'd shredded it. She tossed the ribbon aside and started with a new one.

"There, that looks nice." Mary Kate admired a full tray of favors and deftly moved it out of reach of her daughter's hands. "I love doing things like this." She flashed a smile, much like her father's. "I'm glad we're doing this together."

"Me, too." Stacy added. She picked up the tray. "I'll put these in the kitchen."

"I don't suppose she's done many things together with a family," Siobhan said softly as the door closed behind Stacy. "Poor child."

Claire's heart tightened. Would Siobhan pity her, if she knew more about Claire's background? The thought made her hands clench.

"Stacy's going to be all right." That came out sounding more defensive than she intended.

"Of course she is." Siobhan looked a little surprised. "Goodness, you've done wonders with her, Claire. She's so excited about the job you got for her. She can't wait for Monday morning and her first day."

She regretted betraying her feelings, but it was too

late now. What was it about the Flanagans? They brought out all sorts of emotions she'd done without for years.

"I didn't really get her the job. She did that herself. I just helped her get ready, that's all."

"You can take me to your hairdresser any time you want." Mary Kate ruffled her red curls. "I'm ready to get this all cut off."

Under cover of the chorus of protest from Siobhan and Nolie, Claire picked up the iced-tea pitcher and went into the kitchen. The Flanagans got under her guard. Maybe it was the stress of the wedding, bringing feelings to the surface that she thought she'd safely buried a long time ago.

Stacy stood at the counter, looking at her reflection in the microwave. She turned, grinning, at Claire's approach. "I still can't believe it's me."

"You do look different."

That was an understatement. The ragged waif was gone, replaced by a girl whose hair shone and face glowed. She looked—Claire struggled for the comparison she wanted, and then she had it.

Stacy looked loved. Cherished. Funny, how easily you could tell that about a person.

Stacy patted her stomach, just beginning to round. "Pretty soon I'll look pregnant, won't I?" The faintest tremor sounded in her voice.

Claire squeezed her shoulder. "You'll still look great," she said. "Hey, I saw a cute tunic top at the store that would be terrific for the summer. I'll pick up a couple of them for you."

Stacy turned. Before Claire caught her intent, she'd hugged her. "Thanks." Stacy's voice was muffled. "For everything."

Heart aching, she patted the girl's back. "You're going to be okay. I promise."

"Right." Stacy drew back and carefully blotted the tears that had been about to spill over. "Don't know why I get so weepy sometimes."

"Pregnancy hormones." Siobhan stood in the doorway with the last tray of favors. "That's all it is."

Stacy nodded. "That's what it said in that book you gave me." She moved to the refrigerator. "I'll take the sandwiches in now. I bet the guys are getting hungry."

"They're always hungry," Siobhan said, moving out of the way as Stacy pushed through the swinging door. She smiled at Claire as the door closed. "She really is going to be all right, you know."

"I hope so." She shook her head. "One minute I'm happy about the way she looks, and the next I'm worried about it because if Ted sees her, her appearance might make his behavior worse."

"I know." Siobhan patted her shoulder in much the same way she'd tried to reassure Stacy. "I've wasted a lot of energy in my time trying to cope with things that hadn't happened yet. Don't you do that."

Irrationally, she felt better. "I'll try not to."

"Good." Siobhan picked up a full tea pitcher. "You're doing a good thing with that girl, Claire. Please, don't second-guess yourself about it."

She followed Stacy toward the dining room, dodging Brendan as she went through the swinging door.

He held the door for her and then let it swing closed. "Getting some good advice from my aunt?"

"She is talented in that department." Claire tweaked a bow on one of the favors. That was better than looking into Brendan's eyes and wondering what he was feeling. "She kind of reminds me of my mother."

"How so?" Brendan hoisted himself onto the scrubbed oak table, obviously prepared to stay and talk awhile.

She shrugged, uncomfortable with the subject even though she was the one who'd brought it up. "I don't know. Having a gift for making a home, I guess. The talent passed me by."

She glanced around the kitchen, its countertops cluttered with all the stuff that was dropped by a busy family. The cabinets were a warm pine, and pots of herbs overflowed the windowsills. This kitchen really was the heart of the home. The cliché struck her with its truth.

"Don't sell yourself short in that department. You just haven't had as much practice."

And she never would. The thought struck her as terribly lonely, somehow. More Flanagan influence, no doubt.

"Nolie's going to be part of this." The thought was out before she considered how it sounded.

"I guess she is." Brendan slid off the table, the movement bringing him too close to her. "That's part of marriage—becoming part of a whole new family." His voice deepened. "You know, Gabe and I have always been close. Closer than brothers, really."

She risked a glance up at him. His face was very intent, his eyes serious.

"The first time I saw the way Gabe looked at Nolie, I knew how it was going to be with them." He gave a lopsided smile. "I have to confess, I felt jealous. Things wouldn't be the same with Gabe and me."

"Do you still feel that way?"

"Sometimes," he admitted. "But when I see how happy he is, I can't begrudge that. And now I have Nolie as well." His smile grew. "That's worth a lot, isn't it?"

He recognized her jealousy for what it was, but he didn't condemn that. He understood.

"It won't be the same." She echoed his words.

"No, I guess it won't. For any of us." He touched her wrist lightly, and she seemed to feel that touch in every separate cell of her body. "Nothing stays the same. Would you want it to?"

She had to struggle to answer over the thudding of her pulse against his hand. "I guess not. But it's hard, even so."

His fingers tightened against her skin. "Maybe that's the real purpose behind all of this wedding hoopla. It helps us make the transition from one relationship to another. All of us, not just the bride and groom."

"So you're finally seeing the value of favors and parties?" She managed a smile.

"You were right about having all the wedding trimmings, okay? I confess." His face lightened. "I admit I didn't know it all."

If she looked into his smiling eyes any longer, someone would have to wipe her off the floor with a sponge. "I'm glad you finally see that." She pulled her hand away, feeling as if she left part of herself behind. "Never underestimate the power of a woman."

"Hey, I already gave in, didn't I?" He held the door for her and then followed her into the dining room. "My aunt Siobhan taught me that."

Siobhan, putting sandwiches out on the table, looked up at that with a warm smile, and Claire became choked with emotion again. Like it or not, these people were having an effect on her. The question was, could she go back and be content with who she was once all this was over?

Brendan shoved the porch swing with one foot and groaned. "I ate too much. As always when I'm here."

Stacy, sitting next to him, polished off the last crumbs of her slice of cake with her finger. "Your aunt is really a good cook. She's teaching me how to make some things, too. I never learned anything like that before."

"That's good."

He found he was exchanging glances with Claire, who occupied the bentwood rocker opposite him. Claire was probably thinking what he was—that Stacy had been shortchanged in the parenting department. Or was Claire remembering her own growing-up years without a mother to guide her?

"I could stand some lessons, too," Claire said. "About the only thing I make is broiled chops and baked potatoes. You don't have to think too much about those."

Stacy looked down at her hands. "I tried to call my mother again today. I wanted to show her my new haircut and tell her about my job. But she's still not there."

He pushed back the wave of anger at a mother who'd just go off without a thought in the world for the well-being of her child. "I'm sure she'll come back soon. She'll be happy when she hears about your job."

"Sure she will," Claire added.

Stacy's mouth twisted. "I guess."

He put his hand over hers. "Hey, what's going on? You can tell us." He sensed Claire leaning forward in her chair and felt a flood of support from her.

"Nothing," Stacy mumbled. "It's just—" She put her hand protectively over her stomach in what was probably an unconscious gesture. "If my mom hadn't been stuck with me, maybe her life would have been different. Maybe my dad would have stayed around. She always says he's the only man she ever loved, and he left because of me."

His fingers tightened on hers, and he had to battle the rage before he could speak. "It's not your fault." That came out louder than he intended, and Stacy looked up at him, startled. "What your parents did or didn't do is not because of you. They have to carry that responsibility themselves."

"Yeah, but—"

"No buts." He could hear the passion in his voice, and he knew that Claire heard it, too. "Listen, if you don't remember anything else I've ever told you, remember this. Your parents made bad decisions before you were even born. They've gone on making bad decisions, but that's not your fault."

Claire leaned forward until their knees were touching. She put her hand on theirs, and hers was cool and comforting.

"Brendan's right, Stacy. They made a lot of mistakes, but none of them were because of you. And now you have a chance to make the right choices. You don't have to be angry with them anymore, but you also don't have to make the same mistakes they did."

Stacy took a moment to process that. "Yeah. You're right. I can do the right thing for my baby." She stood, brushing away tears with the back of her hand. "Guess I'll go help Siobhan finish up the dishes." A smile trembled for a moment on her lips. "Thanks."

The screen door slammed behind her. All he could do was stare at Claire. "Did that go all right or not? I couldn't tell."

"I think so. She's still figuring it out, but I think she's on the right track." She studied his face, her deep brown eyes serious. "You got pretty vehement about her not blaming herself for her parents' mistakes."

"She shouldn't."

"No. I just wondered why that pushed your buttons so much."

Claire was the one who pushed his buttons. She was implying that his advice to Stacy was governed by something in his relationship with his parents.

He managed a casual shrug. "Maybe we all have things in our past that affect what we think and say. You told Stacy she could forgive her parents. Have you forgiven yours?"

For a moment, Claire didn't move. Then she got up, spun on her heel and stalked into the house.

He almost launched himself off the swing to follow her. He should apologize, say it was none of his business, say he was sorry. It wouldn't do any good. He'd just proved what he'd been telling himself all along—that he couldn't risk involvement with Claire. It was too easy to hurt her.

He'd have to find another way to work off his guilt, because getting any closer to Claire was not an option.

"Thanks for everything, Siobhan." Claire paused at the door on her way out, her mind running through the lists of things that had needed to be done for the shower. "I think it's all ready except for the last-minute things."

"We'll take care of those after church tomorrow." Siobhan enveloped her in a hug before Claire could guess her intent. "Why don't you join us for the service? We can come straight here afterward to finish up."

*No.* The word she wanted to say would be a rude response to the woman's kindness. "I'll see," she evaded. "If I don't make it to church, I'll meet you here afterward."

Siobhan nodded, apparently satisfied with that answer. "Tomorrow, then."

Claire turned away. She stopped, the path to her car blocked by a pick-up basketball game taking place in the driveway. It seemed to be Gabe and Seth against Brendan, Terry and Ryan.

Gabe shot the ball and winced when Terry deflected it from the basket. His gaze caught hers.

"Hey, Claire, we need some help. I'm stuck with just Seth. Come on, be on my team."

"I don't think basketball is Claire's thing," Brendan said, wiping his forehead with the back of his hand. "It's a little rough-and-tumble for her."

"So that's what you think, is it?" The desire to prove him wrong got the better of her. She put down her bag. "Toss that ball here, Gabe."

Gabe, grinning, shot the ball to her. "Go get 'em, Claire."

She dribbled toward Ryan. He hesitated, obviously not sure he should block her the way he would his sister. She took advantage of his momentary lapse to dribble around him. Brendan tried to block too late. She went up for the shot, hearing the satisfying swish when she made it.

She grinned at the stunned faces. "Girls varsity state champs, two years in a row." Before she'd let her personal life get out of control.

She snatched the ball as Brendan made a grab for it. "Now, you guys still want a game?"

Brendan jostled her, almost knocking the ball lose. "You got it. Give us your best shot."

Good thing she'd worn jeans and sneakers today. They weren't as comfortable as the shorts Terry wore, but at least she could play. She'd show Brendan—

What would she show Brendan? This wasn't about him. It was just a game. She was not trying to get at him for his remark about her parents.

Maybe so, but she'd forgotten how quickly personalities came out on a basketball court. That the court was just a basket mounted over the garage doors didn't matter.

Gabe was take-charge, directing his small team with a wave of his hand or a nod, feeding her the ball once he saw the strength of her shot. She hadn't lost her skill, even after all these years, and it felt good to push her body once again.

Seth played with concentration, but he was clearly not as competitive as his brothers. He'd slide back and let someone else take the shot, and he was always ready with an encouraging word.

Ryan was quick and flashy, probably wanting to show up his big brothers. Terry, tough and scrappy. She'd grown up outnumbered by brothers, and she had to prove she was just as tough.

And Brendan. She'd better concentrate on the game instead of on Brendan, but that was easier said than done. He played basketball the way he did everything—with single-minded concentration. He was a tough competitor, and he probably played more often than his cousins did.

"No fair." Gabe leaned over to catch his breath after Brendan jostled past him to make a shot. "You're getting in too much practice with those juvenile delinquents of yours."

Brendan dribbled, grinning at him, a lock of dark hair falling in his eyes. His skin glowed with exertion. "They don't play by the rules, believe me. This is a tea party compared to playing with them."

"Tea party, is it?" Claire snatched the ball away while he was still looking at Gabe. "We'll see what kind of tea party this is."

She dribbled toward the basket, feeling him close behind her. As he reached out to block her shot she fed the ball to Seth, who went up and dunked it, grinning.

She spun out of Brendan's way as he came down, her foot slipping. If she put herself out of commission for the sake of a stupid game—

Brendan grabbed her, his arms closing around her and keeping her upright. She was tight against his chest, and she felt the heat of his breath on her cheek and the pounding of his heart against her hand. Her own heart seemed to beat in rhythm with his.

Oh, no. She tried to push herself away, but her muscles seemed to have lost any will. She could only cling to him and face the truth.

What she felt for Brendan wasn't friendship, no matter how much she might try to convince herself of that. She loved him. She couldn't kid herself any longer. She loved him, and there was no future in that at all.

## Chapter Eleven

Claire fished in her bag and pulled out a bill to put in the offering plate that was coming down the pew. If anyone had told her a month ago that she'd be sitting in church with the Flanagan family on a Sunday morning, she'd have said they were crazy.

Well, this was a special event, sort of like part of the wedding preparations, with the shower this afternoon. She hadn't liked to go on refusing invitations when Siobhan was so helpful with the wedding. Besides, coming this morning provided an opportunity to see what the sanctuary looked like filled with people.

She'd just given herself a few too many reasons for her actions. The truth was, she'd been—well, curious, she supposed. She'd wanted to see what Brendan was like in action.

She had to admit he looked imposing in that black robe. She'd thought initially that the height of the pulpit gave him an unfair advantage, letting him look down on everyone. But then when the sermon began he'd left the pulpit, moving down to their level to speak without notes.

She'd arrived this morning determined to remain unaffected by what happened here, but things hadn't worked out quite that way. Brendan had spoken, openly and without what she'd thought of as preaching, about what loving one's neighbor really meant. And she had discovered she couldn't remain unaffected by the service after all.

Brendan obviously cared about what he was saying. It meant so much to him that his passion had reached out to her, shaking her with the realization of how little she'd cared for anyone in a long time.

She'd once thought her detachment was an advantage, but she knew now that it wasn't a good way to live. Even if she never saw Brendan again after the wedding, she'd take something good away from having known him.

The congregation stood for the final hymn, and she stood with them. She took the side of the hymnal Siobhan held out to her. The music soared upward to the arched ceiling, seeming to lift spirits, too.

They'd known what they were doing, those people who'd designed gothic churches. Every line of the sanctuary drew the eye and the mind upward. Even someone like her, a rational being who wasn't looking for spiritual inspiration, could appreciate that.

The hymn came to an end. Brendan held his arms out

to his congregation, as if he'd embrace every one of them. His smile touched her, evoking an answering smile.

"Walk closely with God. Love your neighbor, even the least lovable. And don't forget to give thanks."

The organ music swelled to fill the sanctuary, and the service was over. Claire closed the hymnal, stepped into the aisle and found herself face-to-face with Harvey Gray.

One of her basic principles in dealing with her employer was never to be caught by surprise. Or at least, never to show it.

"Good morning, Mr. Gray." She tried to smile as if it were the most common thing in the world to encounter him in the aisle of Grace Church.

"Ms. Delany." He wore what she thought of as his lean and hungry look. "I'm surprised to see you here. I didn't realize you attended church."

And what are you doing in my church again? That was Gray's unspoken question. He'd made it clear, the night he'd found her with Brendan's teens, that he didn't approve of her connection with that project. He was used to having even his most implicit wishes followed.

"Harvey, how are you this morning?" Siobhan squeezed around Claire to take his hand.

"Fine, thank you, Siobhan." He turned on his social smile as he shook hands with Siobhan and Joe.

She shouldn't be surprised that they knew each other. They'd belonged to the same church for years and Joe Flanagan was pretty high up in the fire department, from what she understood. That had importance attached to it, if not social status—Harvey Gray knew everyone who was anyone in Suffolk.

Someone else caught Gray's attention, and she slipped quickly up the aisle, not waiting for Siobhan. She'd see them at the house. Right now she needed to do some damage control. If her boss wasn't happy to see her here, then she'd disappear from view.

She'd nearly reached the back of the sanctuary when someone caught her arm. She turned, trying to place the girl who stood between her and the door.

"I'm Amy Wagner," she said helpfully. "I was here the night you were teaching us about interviewing and stuff, remember?"

One of Brendan's teens. "Of course," she said untruthfully. She'd managed to block most of that disastrous night out of her thoughts, including the faces of the kids. "How are you?"

"Okay. Listen." The girl's grip tightened, as if Claire had threatened to flee. "Some of us were talking to Stacy. About her new job and all. And we were thinking—well, maybe you'd give it another shot."

"Another shot?"

The girl shrugged. "Well, you know. Teach us about getting jobs and all. You think?"

She'd like to say no and get out as fast as her legs would carry her. She had enough to do with Stacy and the wedding, to say nothing of her job.

Unfortunately, some of the words from Brendan's sermon seemed to have taken up residence in her mind.

"God doesn't expect all of us to become Mother Teresa," he'd said. "God just expects that you'll do the good works He puts in front of you to do."

She wasn't one of Brendan's flock. She didn't have to follow his advice. But she'd been thinking about how she'd changed, and the girl was looking at her like a puppy that expected to be kicked.

"All right." The words were out before she could reconsider. "I'll talk to Reverend Flanagan about setting something up."

"Cool. I'll be there." Amy turned and whipped back down the aisle as if she feared Claire would change her mind if she stuck around.

It was another commitment to add to her long list. She dared a glance back to where she'd last seen her boss to find him deep in conversation with someone, his back to her. Good. At least he hadn't seen her talking with the girl.

One session, that's all she'd agree to. With a little luck, Gray would never know anything about it.

She neared the door, where she could see Brendan greeting his parishioners as they exited. Up close, the black robe made him seem older, different, maybe a little more distant. It hadn't bothered her when he'd been in the pulpit, but she wasn't quite sure how she'd have a normal conversation with him while he was wearing it.

For one brief moment her treacherous mind presented her with the image of a different Brendan—a Brendan who was flushed and sweaty, holding her tightly against the T-shirt he'd worn to play basketball. A Brendan she'd looked at and known that she loved.

No. She was not going to think that. It was impossible. It couldn't be true. The feeling was a random infatuation brought about by the orange blossoms in the air.

The line moved a few steps closer to the vestibule, and she took a deep breath. A quick greeting, and she'd scoot on out the door. That was all, and when they were at the shower this afternoon, she'd be too busy even to notice him.

Brendan bent courteously over to talk to a pair of tiny elderly ladies who must be sisters, they looked so much alike. He had a patient ear for each of them, while she shuffled her feet and wondered if she could be rude enough to brush past them.

Finally they moved on. She was ready with a quick handshake and a smile. She wasn't ready for Brendan to clasp her hand in both of his.

"Claire, you came. I'm so glad."

"Your aunt talked me into it." She would not let herself think about how warm and strong his grasp was. "We're heading over to the house right away to get ready for the shower, and we don't have much time."

She started to pull her hand free. But Brendan's grip was firm, and the elderly women had stopped at the top of the outside steps, carrying on an animated conversation with someone beyond them without noticing that they effectively blocked the doorway.

"That's good. I'll see you over there." His grasp tightened. "There's something I wanted to say to you first." He lowered his voice, but the elderly women weren't paying attention, and the people behind Claire had come to a halt for conversation as well. "I'm sorry."

"For what?" Not for making me care about you, by any chance?

His brows drew down. "I said something that hurt you yesterday. I'm sorry."

His words popped back into her mind. "You were wrong about my parents." And if he wasn't, she certainly wouldn't admit it. "But I guess I started it by mentioning yours." They'd both hit sore spots, obviously.

"I lost my temper." He said it as if confessing the gravest of sins. "That should never have happened."

She studied his face. "If that's an example of losing your temper, all I can say is that it wasn't visible to anyone else. In fact, I don't think I've ever seen you lose your temper. Don't you have one?"

She'd said the words lightly, not thinking about anything but the fact that he still grasped her hands. But she was looking in his eyes, and what she saw there shook her to her soul.

Torture. That was all she could see. Brendan's eyes looked tortured, and the expression was so strong that it wrenched her heart. Why did he look that way?

"Brendan—"

What could she say? This was obviously a struggle of faith. She couldn't help someone deal with a spiritual struggle when she didn't believe in anything. The people behind her moved up, obviously ready for their turn with the minister. She could only give him a sympathetic look as she went out the door.

Brendan hadn't expected to enjoy the shower. For one thing, it brought him into close proximity with Claire again, which always seemed to have unfortunate results.

And for another, he'd thought the whole idea just a little silly. Why a shower, anyway?

But an hour into the event, he'd begun to see things a little differently. He leaned against the door frame, out of the flow of traffic, and watched as Nolie and Gabe opened presents.

This wasn't about playing childish games, or about giving the wedding couple gifts they'd never use. It was about community, gathered around two of their own to celebrate a significant step in their lives. It pointed people toward the fact that two were about to become one.

Seth, his two-year-old son slung over his shoulder like a sack of potatoes, came to join him. "You look like you're making a sociological study of wedding customs among the natives."

Brendan grinned, tickling Davy, who responded with a giggle. "You're not far wrong. I was thinking this isn't a bad way to get ready for a wedding."

Seth's eyebrows went up. "You don't really believe they need a pasta machine, do you?"

"Well, maybe not. But the gifts are a sign of recognition that a new family is being formed. That's important."

Seth's blue eyes seemed to darken. "To last forever," he said softly.

For a moment Brendan couldn't respond. Good-natured Seth took life so equably that it was easy to forget that he'd lost his wife when Davy was born. However much that grieved him, he usually kept it to himself.

"I'm sorry."

Seth shrugged, his normal easygoing smile returning. "Hey, it's okay. And you're right. Even with the modern trappings, like having couples here, it's still about getting them ready for marriage. Married women passing on their secret recipes, while all the men can do is pound each other on the back and make stupid jokes."

"You think women are better at that sort of thing than we are?"

"Probably." Seth nodded toward Claire, who was leaning over the couch, recording each gift and giver. "Claire's done a great job. I didn't know what to make of her at first, but she's okay."

"You're just saying that because she helped you beat us yesterday."

"She's pretty good. Did she play college ball?"

Brendan shrugged, but actually he knew the answer to that, didn't he? Claire hadn't been playing basketball or going to college dances after high school. She'd been struggling to survive.

Davy yawned, snuggling his face into Seth's shoulder.

"I'd better get this guy down for a nap." Seth elbowed him as he moved past. "If you stand there and stare at the woman like that, someone might get the impression that you're interested."

He went back down the hall before Brendan could respond, even supposing he'd been able to think of something to say. Was he being that obvious? Maybe so.

But it was hard to keep his eyes off a Claire who seemed to have shed all her reserve. With her face alight with laughter over some comment about a gift, she looked years younger than the woman he'd first quarreled with about the wedding plans.

He loved her. He couldn't have her.

That was the truth, expressed as plainly as he knew how. She'd already been nearly destroyed by an abuser. For an instant he seemed to see Claire, cringing away from a blow. Seemed to see his father's face, black with rage, as he struck out at Brendan's mother.

No. He couldn't risk it.

*Why haven't You taken the anger away? I've asked so often. Why don't You answer?*

He knew what he'd tell someone else who asked that question. He'd say that God always answered prayers, but that sometimes, for reasons people can't understand, the answer is no. Oddly enough, that didn't seem like a good enough response when he asked the question himself.

A high sign from his aunt stopped what was becoming a fruitless argument with himself. They were finishing up the gifts, and she wanted all hands on deck to serve the food. He followed her into the kitchen. By the time he got there, she was already pulling bowls of chicken salad from the refrigerator.

"It's going well, isn't it?" She paused long enough to smile at him. "Claire's done a wonderful job."

"Not just me."

Claire came quickly into the kitchen behind him, and his heart tightened in response to her presence.

"Mostly you." Siobhan passed her a bowl and a handful of serving spoons. "You were the only one who could get Nolie to agree, and look how much she's enjoying it."

"She is, isn't she?" Claire's face was radiant with her smile.

If she ever looked at him that way— Well, she wouldn't.

"You've given both of them a day to remember," he said, pushing his feelings aside. "Congratulations, Claire. You were right."

She turned that smile on him, nearly knocking him off his feet. "I'm delighted to hear you admit that."

"Hey, when I'm wrong, I'm wrong." He sounded normal, didn't he? "You've converted me. Weddings deserve all the flourishes."

Siobhan rounded the table and put her arm around Claire, hugging her as if Claire were one of her daughters. "Thank you, Claire. You made this possible."

Tears brightened Claire's eyes as she returned the hug. "Nolie's lucky. She's finally getting the family she's always deserved."

His throat tightened until he couldn't possibly speak. But he didn't need to. Siobhan put her hand on Claire's cheek with a gentle touch.

"You're her family. That makes you part of ours. Don't go away from us when the wedding is over."

Claire blinked the tears away. "I won't." The words were almost a whisper.

Then she cleared her throat, as if embarrassed at the display of emotion. "We'd better get this food out there before they storm the kitchen."

"Right." Brendan seized a basket of rolls in each hand, glad of something to do that covered his emotions. He didn't begrudge Claire her part in the family or the welcome she'd received.

He just wasn't sure how he'd go on seeing her on a regular basis without somehow letting his feelings for her show.

Less than a week to go before the wedding, and she was wasting precious time going to meet with Brendan's teens. Claire frowned at Brendan across the front seat of his car. When he'd called her at work to say he'd set up the meeting, she'd protested that she had to work late, that Monday was her busiest day and that her car was in the shop for service and wouldn't be ready on time.

Brendan had blandly ignored her arguments and said he'd pick her up. So she'd rushed out to the corner to meet him, wondering why on earth she couldn't just tell him no, and whether she'd gotten away without Harvey Gray knowing where she was headed.

She stole a glance over her shoulder at the ornate brick facade of the Gray building receding in the distance. Gray couldn't possibly know. Despite what some of his employees thought, the man didn't have X-ray vision.

"Are you still worried about Harvey Gray's opinion?"

"He's my employer. Of course I worry about what he thinks." Her voice was tart. "And if you don't, you should. Like I said before, he's a dangerous enemy."

"He's not my enemy." Brendan sounded as if he were being tolerant of her foibles. "The church is different."

"The church is composed of ordinary people. You taught me that. And I know how people like Harvey Gray operate. You don't want to get on his bad side."

"The church is a mission, not a business. We run on faith."

"You run on contributions. It's not a good idea to alienate one of your biggest contributors."

Brendan shook his head, smiling.

Maybe it was just as well that his idealism annoyed her so much. It was a reminder of how ill-suited they were to each other.

Not that she needed a reminder. She'd already decided that what she felt for him was nothing more than attraction. Infatuation. It would pass with the wedding, and a month from now she'd look back and laugh at her foolishness.

"The shower turned out great." He must feel that

there were safer topics of conversation. "Nolie was still beaming the last I saw her."

"I know." Her voice softened at the thought of Nolie's happiness. "Well, she deserves all the happiness in the world, and she seems to be getting that with Gabe. As for the shower, a lot of the credit goes to your aunt and cousins. I'd never have gotten it done without them."

"You sound almost surprised. Didn't you think they meant it when they said they'd help?"

She shrugged. "I didn't know. I don't have many women friends."

Brendan stopped for a red light and glanced at her. "Why is that?"

"I don't know." Did he always have to probe for the inner meaning of everything? Anyone who got involved with him would have to get used to total honesty. "I guess I've been too busy with work for that."

"Aren't there other women who work where you do?"

"Not at my level." There was a trace of pride in her voice. "No other woman has ever risen that high."

"I suppose it's hard to make friends with people you consider your subordinates."

She couldn't decide whether that was an insult or not. "Look, my business mentors have all been male. That's just the way it is. The relationships your aunt and cousins have are out of my range of experience. I've always been one of the boys. That's how you get ahead in business."

She realized that her hands were balled into fists.

Brendan certainly had a talent for getting under her skin. If she had a sneaking suspicion that most women were weak, well, that wasn't any of Brendan's business.

The radio crackled to life, cutting off any response Brendan might have made. He listened intently to something that was mostly incomprehensible to her, his face closed. Then he put on his turn signal and veered sharply around a corner.

She grasped the armrest, alarmed. "What is it?"

"Multivehicle accident with injuries and a chemical spill on the bypass. I'll have to go." He touched a switch, and a siren she hadn't known existed wailed. "I have to go straight there. My gear is in the trunk. You can drop me and then take my car to the church."

She wanted to protest, but she couldn't. This grim-faced, take-charge man was a Brendan she hadn't known existed. All she could do was hang on for the ride.

# Chapter Twelve

She ought to leave, but somehow she couldn't. Claire got out of the car slowly, horrified by the scene in front of her. A tractor trailer and a car had collided, with the semi spilling barrels of some unidentifiable liquid on the road. Yellow-coated firefighters swarmed around the wreckage, and the swirling lights of police cars and fire trucks added to the sense of urgency.

"Claire, what are you doing here?" Joe Flanagan, in yellow jacket and helmet, approached her. His bulldog face bore more than its usual share of worry lines.

"I was in Brendan's car when he got the call, so I had to come with him. He told me to take his car and go on to the church, but I couldn't." She hoped he didn't think she was motivated by morbid curiosity.

"I know how you feel." Joe's gaze was on the firefighters, not her. "I'm supposed to be sitting at my desk at headquarters, but I never can manage that when something big is going down." He glanced at her. "Don't tell Siobhan I was here, okay?"

She nodded. "I won't get you in trouble."

"It's not that." His grin flickered. "Well, not entirely. Siobhan never shows that she's worried, but it takes a lot out of her."

"I know." She'd seen it.

The flicker of humor left his face. "I never realized how much until my heart attack. I think it's worse being at home imagining what's happening than being here."

Siobhan had sought refuge in prayer when Claire had been with her the last time her family had been in danger. Now Claire was seeing the situation from the other side.

"Does it help? Being here, I mean, when your family's out there."

She'd already spotted both Ryan and Seth among the helmeted figures. And Brendan, of course. She couldn't take her eyes off him. Her stomach cramped.

"It doesn't help unless I can be in there with them." Joe's tension was palpable. "Look, they're going to lay down foam. That'll let them get to the car."

Claire's throat tightened. The car was barely identifiable, crunched under the body of the truck. "Can anyone possibly have survived that?"

"You'd be surprised at what people come through."

*Please.* She wasn't praying, was she?

Gravel crunched under heavy footsteps. A state police officer approached, his eyes invisible behind his dark glasses. "You'll have to move on, Miss."

"She's with me," Joe said.

She couldn't imagine that would work, but apparently Joe had influence. The man stalked on past them, not breaking his stride.

She spotted a flurry of activity around the remains of the car, and then one of the firefighters gestured broadly.

"Someone's alive in there," Joe interpreted. "The paramedics are going in." The faintest quaver in his voice alerted her. He meant Terry was going in.

"She—" She stopped, her voice choking. "How can you stand it?"

He shrugged. "Terry's my little girl. But she's one of the best, too. She has to do her job."

Terry's figure, slender even in the protective gear she wore, began to squirm under the truck. Then someone else followed her—someone Claire would have recognized no matter how much gear he had on. A cold hand gripped her heart.

"Brendan's going in, too."

Joe nodded. "Bren never holds back if someone's in trouble, no matter how dangerous. He might be the last spiritual comfort for a dying person."

He said it almost matter-of-factly, as if she should have known that about Brendan.

Maybe she had. Maybe at some level she'd already realized that behind Brendan's mild exterior was a core of strength that couldn't be denied. He wouldn't back away from danger if he thought he could help another human being.

Her hands clenched until her nails bit into her palms. "They're in danger, aren't they?"

He nodded, his jaw tight. He lifted a walkie-talkie she hadn't realized he was holding and said something into it. A burst of static answered him, but he seemed to understand. His expression grew even grimmer.

He muttered something that might have been a prayer under his breath. "Those power lines are live. One loose spark, and things could go sour in a hurry."

"Can't they shut down the power?" She could hear the horror in her voice. All those people—they really were risking their very lives. Brendan. Terry. "Shouldn't they wait until it's safe?"

"Whoever is in that car could be dead by then." Joe gripped her arm. "Look. There's Terry. She's signaling for a stretcher. They're going to try bringing someone out."

Claire held her breath, watching as the stretcher was maneuvered under the truck into what seemed an impossibly small space. The dangling power lines swung in the light breeze, too close.

*Please, please.* She could hardly deny now that the words were a prayer. *If You're really there, You know that they're in danger. Protect them, please.*

Joe's fingers gripped her arm, as if some human link was necessary to keep him sane while those he loved were in peril. He didn't speak, but she sensed he was praying.

Moments passed; the power lines swung and crackled. The bulk of the truck loomed over the struggling figures like some prehistoric beast ready to spring.

*Please.*

She could see movement under the truck. She bit her lip, her whole being straining as if she'd rush forward to help.

*Please.*

Then Terry emerged, reaching behind her to pull out the stretcher. Other people grabbed it, and the stretcher was free of the wreckage. Brendan slid out behind it.

"Careful, careful," Joe whispered. "Don't relax. You're not clear of the lines yet."

They moved with quick precision, a couple of people on each side of the stretcher. That was Brendan, bending over the still figure. He was holding the person's hand.

Her heart seemed to stop beating. Smoothly, moving in unison, they cleared the deadly arc of the power lines. They rolled the stretcher swiftly toward the waiting emergency vehicle.

Joe's grip loosened. "They're out. They're safe. Thank God."

"Yes." They were safe. That was what mattered, not whether she'd said an involuntary prayer to a God she wasn't sure she believed in.

She took a deep breath. "Maybe I should leave. I'm supposed to be at the church to meet with the kids at the drop-in center."

She didn't want to be here if Terry and Brendan came over to talk to Joe. Her ridiculous assumptions about the Flanagan women had come back to haunt her.

She'd been so wrong about them. She hadn't recognized the sheer courage it took for Terry to do what she did. Or the courage Siobhan displayed every day, knowing the ones she loved were in danger.

She definitely didn't want to see Brendan right now, because she wasn't sure at this moment that she could keep him from knowing how she felt about him.

"Thanks, Seth." Brendan raised his hand in a farewell wave as his cousin drove off after dropping him at the church. Even the simple gesture took an effort. He was bone-tired, the fatigue as much spiritual as physical.

They'd all come close today—he and Terry especially, but the others, too. The situation could so easily have gone sour.

But they'd all walked away from it. Chalk another one up to the legendary Flanagan luck, although if pressed, he'd have to say he didn't believe in luck. A firefighter walked away because he or she was well-trained, well-equipped and had a lot of people on his side praying.

Had Claire been praying today, when she'd stood with Uncle Joe along the side of the highway, watching, her hands clasped, her body tense? She probably wouldn't admit to it.

His mind and body had been totally engaged in the work that had to be done. No one knew better than he did how terrifying and dangerous it had been under that semi. A person couldn't do that and think of anything else.

But beyond thought was instinct. Even when he hadn't looked in Claire's direction, he'd been aware of her. It was as if he were hardwired to know where she was.

He pushed open the door to the office wing, noting that his car was parked at the curb. Had Claire just dropped it off and left, or had she actually worked with the kids? She'd so obviously not wanted to do that, and he still wasn't sure if that reluctance came from her fear of what Gray would think or something else.

Voices came from Fellowship Hall, and then a burst of laughter. He swung the double door open, and several faces turned toward him.

Claire was there, along with Amy Watson, Stacy and five other kids. Not a huge turnout, but it was a start, at any rate.

More importantly, the atmosphere seemed relaxed. Claire actually looked as if she were enjoying herself. She'd shed her suit jacket, and her usually impeccable bronze hair was tumbling around her face.

"Hey, Rev." Stacy grinned at him. "You're late."

"I had other business." He pulled out one of the folding chairs and propped his foot on it, leaning his elbow on his knee. If he actually sat down, he just might sleep there all night. "Don't let me interrupt you."

"We're actually finished." Claire pushed a tendril of hair back from her face, as if his presence had made her aware that it was disarranged. "Most of the kids left half an hour ago, but we were talking."

"How did it go?" How are you, Claire? What were you thinking when you stood and watched the rescue today?

"Great." Amy answered for her. "I'm gonna get a job, you wait and see. Maybe even save up enough money to get into the Licensed Practical Nurse program."

"Sounds good." He glanced at his watch. How had it gotten to be nearly seven? Claire was probably starved. "Maybe we ought to call it a night. Stacy, do you need a ride home?"

She shook her head. "Amy's going to drop me." She stood, collecting some papers from the table. "Thanks, Claire."

"Yeah, thanks," Amy echoed.

With a few backward glances, they filed out. He heard the outside door bang shut behind them.

"So, how did it really go? Did they give you any trouble?" He was spinning it out, trying for a little more time with Claire even though he knew it was a bad idea.

"Well, Rick was his usual obnoxious self, but I think even he got something out of it." She shuffled some papers together, and he realized they were job application forms. She must have brought them for the kids to practice on.

"It's good of you to go to this much trouble." He tapped the stack of papers. "Even if we did push you into it."

Her face was turned partially away from him, but he

thought she smiled. "Well, some people can be pretty persuasive."

"You're talking about Amy, I presume."

"Of course." She glanced at him, eyes like brown velvet. "How did it go for you? The person you took to the hospital—is he going to be all right?"

"She," he corrected. "Multiple injuries, including a broken pelvis, but she'll make it." He grimaced. "She was talking on a cell phone. She's paying a high price for a moment's inattention."

"It could have been worse." Emotion flared in her eyes. "Someone else could have paid the price. You, or Terry, or one of the others."

He had to take her hand. He couldn't help himself. Her fingers curled around his, clinging.

"We didn't. We all walked away. Uncle Joe would call it the famous Flanagan luck in action."

She shook her head slightly. "I was with him. I don't think he was relying on luck."

"No, probably not." What about you, Claire? Did you pray for us?

Her grip tightened. "Do you take chances like that often?"

"Not often, no." He shrugged. This was something civilians didn't understand. "The thing is that you never know. The most routine call can turn deadly in an instant, so you always have to be ready."

"You didn't have to go under that truck." She looked almost angry with him.

"Yes. I did." He studied her face. "That woman needed the reassurance that someone was there praying for her." He managed a grin. "Besides, I couldn't let my little cousin show me up."

"Terry was amazing. I couldn't believe she was making wedding favors one day and dragging someone out from under a tractor trailer the next."

"She's good. They all are. I'd rather have Seth heading up a team than anyone else I know."

"The heroic Flanagans," she said softly.

He might almost imagine Claire admired him. His stomach twisted, reminding him. She wouldn't, not if she knew the truth about him.

She was so close, her face inches from his. The smallest movement could bridge the distance between them.

He couldn't. He couldn't risk a relationship with Claire, knowing what he did about himself. And he couldn't tell her. For an instant he imagined her recoiling in horror. No, he'd never tell her. This was his private battle.

"It's getting late." He straightened, putting some space between them. "Shall I drive you home?"

She turned away, her shoulders stiff. "I have to pick up my car at the garage. I can call a cab." She started toward the door.

"I'll drop you." He followed her, reaching around her to push the heavy door.

"You don't have to—" She stepped into the hallway and the words trailed off.

Ted stood there, leaning against the outside door, arms crossed. He'd obviously been waiting for them.

Claire didn't show any obvious signs of tension, but he could feel it, as if her nerve endings touched his. He let the door swing closed, taking his time, and turned toward Ted.

*Father, help me to remember that this is one of Your children, no matter how wrong he may be.*

"Ted." It took an effort to keep his voice neutral. "Can I do something for you?"

The boy jerked a nod. "Tell me where Stacy is. You must know. Or she does." Ted's angry gaze moved to Claire, and his fists clenched.

Brendan shifted his weight so that he was close enough to let his hand brush Claire's, which was pressed tightly against her side. Let me handle this, Claire. Please.

"I know where Stacy is. She's staying at a safe place." He'd leave Claire out of this if he could.

"She's not at a shelter. I asked around."

Ted had shown more persistence than he'd given him credit for. "No, she isn't at a shelter. She has friends to protect her now." He gestured toward his office. "Why don't you come into the office and have a cup of coffee? We'll talk about this whole situation."

Ted took a step as if he'd bar their way if they tried to move past him. "I don't want to talk, Rev. I just want to find Stacy. You don't have any right keeping her away from me." He glared at Claire. "Neither does she."

"I'm Stacy's friend." Claire's voice was as cool as if

she discussed the most recent sales figures, but against his hand her pulse jumped and pounded. "I'm only doing what she wants in not telling you where she is. You've knocked her around for the last time. She's done with you."

"No. She can't be." Ted's face twisted. "I heard. Somebody was talking. They said she's pregnant. She's going to have my kid."

He heard a sharp intake of breath from Claire. Her mind was probably racing just as fast as his was. Still, he'd known all along the news couldn't be kept from Ted forever.

"That's just gossip." Claire got in before he could say anything. "People say stupid things."

Ted took a threatening step toward them. "Is it true? She is going to have a kid?"

"No." Claire's tone was sharp. She wouldn't hesitate a moment to lie for someone she cared about.

"Rev? You tell me the truth. Is she?"

Claire might be able to justify the lie. He couldn't, and even if he could, it was futile. Ted would find out. They had to deal with his knowing sooner or later.

"Yes. She is."

"Where is she?" Ted shook his head slowly, like a bull before it charged. "You tell me where she is. I got a right to know if she's gonna have my kid."

"Why would we tell you?" Claire jerked her hand away from his. "So you can hit her again? Knock her around so badly she loses the baby?"

The pain in her voice cut into Brendan's heart. She knew what she was talking about.

"No! You crazy?" Ted shook his head. "I wouldn't do anything like that. I just want to see her. Make things right."

"The only way you can make things right is to leave Stacy alone." He reached toward the boy. "Come on, Ted. Let's sit down and talk about this."

"Leave me alone. I have to see her."

"Come on—"

Ted swung, knocking his hand away. The anger surged, dark and deadly. He saw his father's fist coming at him—

No. That was a long time ago. His hands curled into fists, and his breath was harsh in his throat. He took a deep breath. He wouldn't let the anger control him.

"That decision's not yours to make, Ted." No one would know the effort it cost to speak naturally. "You hurt Stacy, and she doesn't want to have anything more to do with you. It's time to accept that."

Ted's head swung slowly back and forth. If only he could connect with the boy, make him understand. *Please*—

Ted turned and bolted from the church, the outer door slamming shut behind him.

Despair settled deep into Brendan's soul. He should have been able to help the boy. He'd failed, and Ted was left with no one who cared enough to steer him in the right path.

"I'm sorry."

He didn't realize he'd said the words aloud until Claire swung her head to look at him. Her eyes were so dark with anger that the emotion might almost have been hatred.

"Sorry for what? That you didn't hold the abuser's hand a little longer?" Her fury was so hot it nearly burned him.

"Claire, don't. I wasn't trying to coddle Ted. I just wanted to help him see the right thing to do."

"By telling him Stacy's pregnant? Sure, that'll solve matters for them."

"He would find out anyway. Stacy isn't planning to leave town. Sooner or later he'd know."

"You'd rather he heard it from you."

Maybe she'd never be able to understand how he saw this. She identified too completely with Stacy. He knew why, and he didn't blame her, but—

"The only way I can get anywhere with these kids is by being completely honest. If I start lying, I become just like everyone else who's let them down."

She made a short, sharp gesture, as if rejecting his words. She took a breath, obviously trying to calm herself enough to speak rationally.

"All right. I don't agree, but the damage is done now. He knows. Now what do we do?"

"He may come back and talk to me once he's cooled down. After all, I'm his link with Stacy. Maybe I can make him see that he has to let her go."

Claire gave him a look that suggested he was too

naive to be allowed out without a keeper. "I wouldn't want to be on the chance that will happen. And he's bound to think of the Flanagans sooner or later. He'll go after her."

Well, at least he didn't have to worry about her thinking of him as a hero any longer.

"No one at the house will let him in to see her if she doesn't want to."

"She has a job. She goes out in public. We can't hide her."

"We shouldn't if we could." Didn't she see the obvious answer? "Claire, sooner or later Stacy is going to have to sit down in a room with Ted and settle this situation."

"No!" Her face twisted, the emotions so near the surface that she obviously couldn't help it. "You can't make her do that."

His heart hurt with the pain this was causing her. *Father, help her. She's hurting so much.*

"You're putting yourself in Stacy's place." He kept his voice soft, longing to touch her but not daring to. "But you faced your abuser, eventually. You found the strength to get out."

"It cost too much." She threw the words at him.

"That won't happen with Stacy. She won't face him alone. We can sit down with them—"

"No." She took a step away from him. "No, I won't make her do that. And I won't let you."

She swung and stormed out of the church, leaving him alone to try and find some semblance of peace amidst the wreckage.

## Chapter Thirteen

Several days had passed, and Claire still found it easier to avoid Brendan as much as possible. *Easy* probably wasn't the right word, with the wedding coming up in two days, but after what had happened with Ted, her feelings were in such a jumble that she couldn't begin to sort them out.

She took a step back from the pew, eyeing the bow she'd just attached to the end post. "Stacy, what do you think? A little longer ribbon trailing down?"

The late afternoon sun streamed through stained-glass windows, touching the white ribbon with shades of gold and red. She'd picked Stacy up after work to come in and decorate the sanctuary. Since nothing else was scheduled for the space tonight or Friday, they could do some of the time-consuming details, leaving the final arrangements on Saturday morning to the florist.

Stacy tweaked the bow and then pulled it off entirely. "Like this." She reshaped it with deft fingers, adding long streamers that touched the floor when she reattached it.

"Very nice." Nicer than anything she'd done, certainly. "You really have artistic talent. Have you thought about a job that would let you use it?"

Stacy gave her the first genuine smile she'd seen since she'd told the girl that Ted knew about her pregnancy. "I used to think I wanted to be a hairdresser, but I was thinking it might be cool to work with a florist. I like working in the store, though. They let me wait on a couple of customers today."

"Great." She was relieved that Stacy finally seemed to be thinking about a future in which she took care of herself. "You have plenty of time to decide, but after-school jobs could let you try out different things."

Stacy twisted the ribbon in her hands. "I'll be showing by the time school starts. Wouldn't be much fun being there, even if I want to go."

It was yet another decision that Stacy needed help with, and she certainly didn't have any easy answers. Her head was already whirling with everything they had to do before the wedding.

"Tell you what." She clasped the girl's hand firmly in hers. "Let's put that on the back burner until we get this wedding over with. Then maybe we can look into some of those programs the counselor told you about for finishing high school. Okay?"

Stacy evaded her gaze. "I was thinking, maybe now that Ted knows, things might be different with him."

"How different?" Exasperation sharpened her tone. "Do you think he's going to turn into the perfect husband and father because he knows you're having a baby?"

Come on, Stacy. Can't we wait until after the wedding to deal with this?

That was what she wanted to say, but it would hardly be fair to tell Stacy that. Naturally she was obsessed with what her future would hold.

"You don't know Ted at all." Stacy flared up suddenly, startling her. "He can be really nice sometimes. Sweet and caring."

Claire dropped the ribbon she was holding onto a padded pew and caught both Stacy's hands in hers, forcing Stacy to look at her. "Do you really believe what you're saying? Do you? Was he sweet and caring when he was hitting you?"

Stacy flushed, trying to evade her gaze. "It wasn't all his fault. Sometimes I'd do something stupid, like burn the hamburgers, and he'd get mad because we didn't have much money and everything costs so much. You couldn't blame him for getting mad."

"I can blame him for hitting you."

Stacy was finally opening up to her, but why did it have to be now? Her head ached with all the things that had to be done.

"He didn't mean to. He'd just lose his temper, that's all."

Something seemed to snap in her at that. "Right. He'd lose his temper and hit you. Stacy, there's never an excuse for hitting someone. He's a bully. He hit you because you wouldn't hit back."

"If we were married—"

She could hardly bear to hear the words. "You think that would make it better? If you were married, he'd be stuck with supporting a wife and child when he can barely support himself. You know that. Would he want to walk the floor all night with a crying baby? Or would he hit again?"

"He'd never hit a baby."

"People do." Her heart seemed to be breaking. "What if he hits you while you're pregnant? You could lose the baby."

I did. But she wouldn't say that.

The door between the sanctuary and the rest of the building creaked open. Brendan was standing there. He'd heard. Their eyes met.

Brendan thought she should tell Stacy about her past, but she couldn't. She couldn't.

"Look, Stacy." She tried for a calm she didn't feel. "Ted's not ready for marriage and neither are you. You're only sixteen."

"That doesn't mean I don't have feelings." Stacy wrenched her hands free, glaring at her.

"I know you do, but—"

"You don't know anything about what it's like to be me." Tears filled Stacy's eyes. "You look down on me because you think I was stupid to get involved with Ted and even stupider to get pregnant."

"Stacy, of course I don't look down on you." Her heart ached. "I care about you. I understand."

"You can't." Stacy shook her head vehemently. "How could you? You've got this perfect house and perfect clothes and perfect life. How could you understand what it's like to be where I am?"

Over the girl's head, Claire's gaze locked with Brendan's. Messages passed between them without the need for words.

You have to tell her.

I can't.

She closed her eyes for a second, blocking them both out. She didn't want to see anyone right now. Not Stacy, who reminded her too clearly of the person she'd once been. Not Brendan, whom she couldn't stop loving even though she knew she had to.

"Stacy—" Brendan's voice broke through her pain.

"No." Claire shook her head at him. "No. You're right. I have to do this."

She looked at Stacy, letting everything she felt show in her eyes. "I do know what it's like to be you, Stacy. Because I was once in exactly the same place you are."

Claire's words hit Brendan as hard as a punch to the stomach, and with just as much visceral pain. She was going to tell Stacy about her past—and it was going to hurt her too much.

He shouldn't interfere. Things were bad enough already between him and Claire. But he couldn't just walk away.

He went to them, pushing aside a bag that overflowed with white ribbon. "You don't have to."

"Yes." Her gaze met his. "I do."

Stacy shook her head. "I don't understand. What are you two talking about?"

"About me." Claire said the words firmly, but he knew how much they had to cost her. "I was a pregnant teenager, like you. I was married to the person who beat me up. I felt as if I didn't have any way out or anyone to turn to. I was like you, Stacy. So I really do understand."

Tears welled in Stacy's eyes. "You? But—what happened to your baby? Did you give it up for adoption?"

The pain that crossed Claire's face was so intense that it seared him, too. He reached out almost involuntarily to clasp her hand. She probably didn't welcome his support, but he had to touch her.

"No. I didn't have a chance." Her voice choked. She took a breath, seeming to force air into her lungs. "He got mad and hit me. Again. He knocked me down a flight of steps."

"No." Stacy's face twisted.

"He stormed out to get drunk with his buddies and left me there. By the time I was able to crawl to get help, it was too late. The doctors tried, but they couldn't save my baby."

Tears poured down Stacy's face. "I'm sorry. Claire, I'm sorry for what I said."

"It's all right."

"I didn't get it. I just thought you were helping me because you thought it was your duty or something. Or because the Rev pushed you into it."

"I didn't even want to help you." Claire managed a smile, somehow, as she put her arm around Stacy. "I knew it would remind me too much. But the Rev is pretty persuasive. Then I got to know you and care about you, and I knew I had to keep you from making the same mistake I did."

"You got married," Stacy said. "You tried to stay with him."

"Yes." Claire's eyes flickered closed for an instant, as if to shut out the pain. "Oh, it wasn't a wedding like Nolie and Gabe are having, in the church in front of all their friends. We just ran away and woke up a justice of the peace who wanted to see our money before he'd perform the ceremony. But it didn't work. It wasn't a real marriage, and two weeks later the beatings started."

Stacy stroked her shoulder and it was as if they'd traded places, so that Stacy was the comforter. "Didn't you have anybody who could help you?"

"I'd quarreled with my father, and I was ashamed to go back and tell him he'd been right. And believe me, my friends dropped me in a hurry when I couldn't do the things they wanted to do anymore."

Oh, Claire. You didn't have the church, because your

father hadn't bothered to keep you in it. And so you didn't realize you could turn to your Heavenly Father for help.

His heart shattered for that confused, hurting girl she'd been.

"I didn't have people like Brendan and his family who cared enough to help." Claire seemed to be thinking along the same lines he was. "I tried to do it all myself, and I lost my baby as a result."

"What happened? How did you get out?"

Claire brushed a lock of hair back from Stacy's tear-stained face with a gentle hand. "I woke up in the hospital and found out the baby was gone. I didn't want to let that little life be lost for no reason, so I decided I had to get out and try to amount to something. It wasn't easy, but I did it. And you can, too."

Stacy mopped at her tears. "I don't think I'm as strong as you."

"You're stronger." Claire squeezed her. "And besides, you have lots of people to help you. Brendan. The Flanagans. Your counselor. Me. You don't have to do it on your own. We won't let you down, will we, Brendan?"

"No." He had to force the word out through a tight throat. "We won't. Promise."

Stacy seemed to straighten, as if she drew strength from their resolve. "Okay. I guess maybe this is going to be all right." She gave a shaky laugh. "I'd better go put some cold water on my face. I didn't mean to cry all over everybody."

"That's okay." He touched her shoulder. "We're here for you, anytime."

He watched as the girl walked quickly out of the sanctuary, her shoulders squared. Then he turned back to Claire, unsure what kind of a welcome he'd get from her now that Stacy wasn't there.

"She sounds as if she's getting it together," he said.

"She'll be up and down plenty more times before she's over this." Claire's voice was calm but her eyes slid away from his, and he knew they weren't okay yet.

Well, he hadn't expected anything more. Claire still blamed him for telling Ted. With her background, he could understand why she felt the way she did.

She'd say he couldn't understand. The image of his father, fist raised, flickered through his mind. But he did understand, more than she'd ever know.

"Well, we just have to be there for her. You're already doing a good job of that. Telling her about yourself— that took a lot of courage, Claire."

Did she understand how much he admired that in her?

She shook her head. "I'm not sure about the courage. There just didn't seem to be anything else to do." She met his gaze, finally. "Strange as it sounds, I'm glad you were here. That made it easier, I think."

There was still a chasm between them that could probably never be crossed, but at least she was looking at him again.

"It's always easier to do something difficult if you have a friend with you," he said carefully.

"Yes." Her face was guarded, but some of the barriers seemed to have vanished. "I'm glad to know I have your friendship."

"Always." It wasn't what he wanted to give her, but it would have to do. "Always, Claire."

If she got through this, she was never going to attend a wedding again. Claire pulled into a parking space at the church Friday afternoon, the back seat of her car filled with boxes of napkins and favors for the reception. She had so much to do, so little time, and today of all days Harvey Gray had decided to keep her late for a little talk.

He'd kept her so long that she'd arrived at the party store moments before they closed. Luckily, they'd had her order ready and waiting for her.

Usually those little talks of Gray's were about work, and she valued that sign that he considered himself her mentor. Today had been different. He'd skirted around the subject, but it had become clear that he'd really wanted to issue a warning on the subject of Brendan Flanagan.

She turned off the ignition and sat staring at the church. It sat squarely on its corner as if it had been there forever. *Decades of tradition,* that was the phrase Gray had used. He felt that Brendan wasn't living up to that tradition.

Brendan might think that Gray's long acquaintance with his family would keep the man from taking any action against him, but if so, he was wrong. She rubbed her forehead. She ought to talk to Brendan about the situation with Gray again. Try to make him see the risk he was running.

Would he listen? Probably not. Stubbornness seemed to be a Flanagan trait. She ought to understand, since she had more than her fair share of it, too.

Well, it would have to wait until after the wedding, like so many other things that were on her mind. She slid out of the car and pulled a couple of boxes out of the back seat. She'd go in through the door that opened into the hallway between the sanctuary and the Fellowship Hall building, so she could take the boxes directly to the kitchen.

Once inside the door she paused, readjusting the precariously stacked boxes. Maybe she ought to leave one here and come back for it. As she bent to set it on the floor, she heard the sound of voices coming from the sanctuary.

The sanctuary door that stood ajar was the one she'd gone through that first night with Brendan, when they'd found Stacy weeping in the pew. That memory must account for the sense of uneasiness that gripped her now.

She tried to shake it off. There were probably dozens of people who had perfectly good reasons for being in the sanctuary. Still, she'd understood no one was using the space until the wedding tomorrow. That was why she and Stacy had decorated yesterday.

It was probably nothing, but still, she couldn't walk away without checking. She stacked the boxes against the wall and opened the sanctuary door.

She couldn't move, couldn't even speak, for fully thirty seconds. The decorations—all those ribbons and flowers she and Stacy had put up so carefully—every one had been ripped from its place. Five boys who should be tossing a basketball in the gym with Brendan were instead throwing the wedding decorations at each other.

While she watched, Rick Romero scooped up an armload of ribbons and pranced down the aisle.

"I'm getting married," he shouted. "Get a load of this."

The sound broke the shock that had held her motionless. "What do you think you're doing?" Fury sent her stalking toward them, fury so strong it felt as if her feet didn't need to touch the ground.

Several of the boys backed up, faces sobering at the sight of her. Rick stood his ground, but he dropped the ribbons.

"We're not doing nothing," he muttered.

"Pick those up off the floor this instant." She stabbed a finger toward the ribbons. "Do you have any idea how much that stuff costs?"

"We were just playing around." Face sulky, he bent to pick up the ribbon. "You don't need to get so mad about it. We didn't hurt anything."

"Didn't hurt anything," she repeated, disbelieving. "Get real, Rick. You're not stupid. You know perfectly well those decorations were for the wedding tomorrow."

Her gaze roved the other faces. She glared at one she recognized from her last session with the kids.

"And you, Jack. You're supposed to be helping with

the reception. Is this your idea of proving you ought to be hired for a job?"

Jack stared at his toes. "Sorry," he mumbled. "I didn't mean to do anything—we just found the door open. We got to fooling around."

"Your fooling around has ruined hours of work." She planted her fists on her hips. "You think saying 'sorry' is going to make that all right?"

"I guess not."

"You've got that right." She didn't know whether she wanted to hit someone or burst into tears. "You—"

"What's going on in here?" The voice came from behind her. She turned to see two figures framed in the doorway.

One was Brendan, looking as horrified as she probably had when she'd walked in. The other was the last person she wanted to see right now.

Harvey Gray.

Gray was the first one to move. He stalked into the sanctuary like a bird of prey looking for something to eat. Or some*one*.

He came to a halt at the end of the center aisle and stood glaring down it. His gaze traveled from the dismantled decorations to Claire's face to the teenagers who huddled closer together, as if for protection.

Rick dropped the bouquet of ribbons on the floor again. Claire winced.

"I don't need to ask the question, do I?" His voice dripped sarcasm. "It's obvious what happened. These juvenile delinquents of the pastor's have wrecked the preparations for the wedding."

She opened her mouth and then closed it again. There really wasn't any proper response to that. They'd done exactly what he said, and she was afraid they'd wrecked more than the wedding decorations.

Gray turned slowly to face Brendan. "I've warned you about this, Flanagan. Now these people are not only in our gymnasium. They're in our sanctuary." He didn't raise his voice, but it came close to quivering with indignation. "Our sanctuary," he repeated.

"We didn't—" Rick began.

It said a lot for the power of Gray's personality that he silenced Rick with a single look. Then he turned back to Brendan.

"End your relationship with these people now. That may be enough to save your pastorate for another year. *May,*" he repeated.

He hadn't raised his voice. People like Harvey Gray didn't need to do that. When you wielded the power he did, a softly spoken warning was enough.

He strode back the aisle, brushing past the boys as if they weren't even there. The door at the rear of the sanctuary slammed shut behind him.

Silence. Claire couldn't think of a single thing to say that would make this any better. Brendan's pastorate here was probably at an end. And she'd be lucky if she came away from this without any permanent repercussions for her career, as well.

As for the kids— She felt a renewed flare of anger. They'd walk away from this without a scratch, of course. What did they care?

"Of all the stupid tricks I've ever seen!" Brendan started toward Rick. Shock reverberated through Claire at the expression on Brendan's face.

Fury—stark, black fury.

She'd never seen him look that way. His fists were doubled, his eyes so dark they looked almost black. Something inside her quailed involuntarily.

The kids seemed to feel it, too. They backed up, as if his anger would sweep them clear out of the sanctuary.

He grabbed Rick by the front of his jacket. "Do you realize what you've done? Do you?"

"Brendan."

She forced his name out through lips that had gone numb with shock. She'd said once that she'd never seen him angry. She couldn't say that anymore.

The kids looked as horrified as she probably did. For an instant she wanted to turn around, run out of the sanctuary, block the image of his face from her mind.

But she couldn't. She touched his arm, and it was hard as steel beneath her hand. "Don't. Brendan, don't. That doesn't do any good."

For a moment longer his fist twisted in Rick's shirt. Then he let go so suddenly, that the boy stumbled back.

Brendan turned a sick, stricken face toward her. His lips moved, as if he wanted to speak but couldn't.

Then he turned and ran out of the sanctuary.

## Chapter Fourteen

For a long moment after Brendan's departure, stunned silence filled the sanctuary. Claire took a shaky breath. Clearly the teenagers were just as shocked as she was over his display of temper.

But it wasn't the anger he'd shown that held her heart in an icy grip. When he'd turned to her, Brendan had looked lost. Totally, completely lost.

Rick shuffled his feet. "Sorry," he muttered.

She had a feeling that was the first completely honest thing he'd said to her.

"I know." She let the words linger for a moment. All the anger she'd felt at them was gone, dissipated in the force of Brendan's emotions. She had to go to him.

But first she had to try and salvage something with these kids.

"I know you're sorry." She kept her voice dispassionate. "Unfortunately, that doesn't solve the problem, does it?"

A couple of head shakes encouraged her that they were at least paying attention.

"The Rev went out on a limb for you, and you let him down. Now he could lose his job." She gestured toward the clutter. "Two people who are important to him are supposed to get married here tomorrow morning. You messed that up, too."

She waited. She hadn't reached them by being angry. Maybe they'd respond to the simple truth.

"We didn't mean anything." Defensiveness colored Rick's words.

"What you meant or didn't mean doesn't change anything. The wedding is still messed up. The Rev may still lose his job."

She expected him to flare up in anger or stamp out. He didn't.

"Well, come on." He turned to the other boys. "You heard. We got to fix all this up the way it was."

Galvanized, they began picking up ribbons. She almost felt like laughing at their expressions. Would have, if the situation hadn't been so serious.

Brendan.

"I'll come back and see how you're getting along in a few minutes."

Several boys nodded, their gazes evading hers. Well, if they were embarrassed at what they'd done, so much the better. She hurried toward the door. Maybe that would make them think twice the next time.

Now for Brendan. She walked quickly down the hall, her whole being straining toward him. But her steps slowed as she neared his office. What could she say to him? He was the one trained to offer advice, not she.

Unfortunately, she was the one who'd seen that uncharacteristic display of anger. And the lost, tortured look that followed it.

She took a deep breath. *Please.*

She wasn't sure who she was asking, or what. She pushed open the door.

Brendan slumped over his desk, head in his hands, his brown hair tousled. He looked up at the sound of her entry, but every line of his body evinced despair.

Carefully, carefully. She had to be even more cautious with Brendan than she'd been with the boys.

"Are you all right?" She approached the desk, longing to reach out and smooth his hair back from his forehead, wanting to say she'd make everything all right.

He shook his head. "I lost control with them. I promised to help them, but I lost control."

"So you lost your temper." She made an effort to keep her voice even. She would not betray just how shocked she'd been when he'd grabbed Rick. "Believe me, they deserved it, the ungrateful little monsters."

He stared at her, his eyes dark with emotion. "You don't understand. I lost control."

She leaned against the desk. "Well, so did I. I was chewing them out when you came in."

"It's not the same." His voice was heavy with a despair she didn't understand.

"Maybe not. My anger didn't seem to impress them. It looks as if yours did." She managed a smile. "You should see them right now. They're trying to put the decorations back up again, and a fine job they're making of it."

Her attempt at humor did nothing to dispel the darkness in his face. He seemed to be unreachable.

She leaned over, caught his wrist and shook it. "Brendan, snap out of it. You lost your temper with them. It's no big deal."

"Yes." His eyes finally focused on hers, and her heart winced at the pain she saw there. "It is a big deal. For me, it's a very big deal."

"Why?" Her fingers tightened as if she'd force the truth out of him. "Tell me what's going on with you, Brendan. Why is losing your temper such a terrible thing?"

For a moment she thought he wouldn't answer. His lips tightened, as if to keep the words in.

"Because." He seemed to choke on the word. "Because it proves I'm just like my father."

She could only stare at him as his words registered. "Your father."

"If you hadn't stopped me, I'd have hurt that boy."

"No." His raw pain flicked at her heart. "You wouldn't have."

"Yes." He shoved his chair back and surged out of it. He turned away from her and paced the few steps to the bookcase. "I would have. I'd have used my fists. Just like my father did."

She saw the truth then. He didn't need to tell her, because she could imagine the whole story.

But he did need to tell her, for his own sake.

"Brendan." She approached him, longing to touch him but not daring to. "Talk to me. Tell me. Your father was an abuser."

She could only be surprised that she hadn't guessed it before from the way he'd reacted.

"He used his fists to settle things." He planted one hand on the bookshelf and leaned his head against his outstretched arm. Every line of his body shouted despair.

"He abused you."

He shook his head. "Not much. Not me. He and my mother—they fought all the time. And every time they fought, it ended the same way. He struck out at her."

"I'm sorry." Her voice was hushed with pain. "Brendan, I'm so sorry."

He raised his head, staring at the books as if he saw something else—something dark and terrible.

"My mother never told anyone. She made me promise never to tell, either."

Don't tell. They were the words that let the abuser go on abusing. "It wasn't fair to put that burden on you."

He didn't acknowledge that she'd spoken. "The day they died they were fighting. I was in the back seat of the car. All I could think was that I hated both of them for the constant arguing."

For an instant he sounded like the boy he'd been then. She could see him so clearly, trapped in the car with the two people he needed to love most in the world.

"They let you down." She felt her way cautiously. "They let each other down, too."

She wasn't sure he even heard what she said. He was lost back in that other time and place.

"I could see it coming. My dad could never keep up with my mother with words. He turned toward her. His face was so angry. He swung at her. His hand—he must have jerked the wheel when he swung. He lost control of the car. We hit the abutment head-on."

She knew the rest of that story. Both of his parents had been killed. That was how he'd come to live with Joe and Siobhan.

"I'm sorry," she whispered.

He straightened, rubbing his face with his hand. He took a breath, and his chest heaved with the effort.

"I never told anyone." He swallowed. "They asked me, afterward, if I knew what caused the car to go out of control. I said I didn't remember. But I did. I do."

She put her hand carefully on his arm. His muscles were painfully taut.

"It was a long time ago. It wasn't your fault."

"I kept thinking, if only I'd found some way to stop them before they started fighting—" His voice broke.

"Oh, Brendan. You can't blame yourself."

"They were fighting about me. Some stupid thing my father wanted me to do and my mother didn't. And I hated them both for using me as an excuse to fight."

"You were a child. You weren't responsible for what they did." She thought her heart would break with his pain.

He shook his head. "I know that. Intellectually, I know that. Inside it's a different story."

She saw what drove him then. "That's why you've tried so hard to help Ted. You can't let the boy go the way your father did."

He didn't deny it. "I couldn't help my father. Maybe I can help Ted."

"Maybe you can."

She took a shaky breath. They'd come a long way from the kids tearing down a few decorations. Her grip on his arm tightened.

"Brendan, I understand why it bothers you, but you still don't need to beat yourself up over losing your temper with the kids."

He shifted, turning so that he could look into her face. His was still dark with pain.

"You don't understand at all. You don't get it, do you? I can't get angry, because I have that same black rage my father did."

"You don't know—"

"Yes, I do. I feel it inside me, waiting to cut loose." His face twisted. "That's why I can't get angry, because if I let the anger take over, I'll lose control entirely. I'll be just like he was."

"No." She could only shake her head, appalled. "You wouldn't. You could never be like that."

"You don't know."

"I do know." She wanted to shake him. "Look at me, Brendan. I'm still here. I'm not running away from you, and of all the people in the world I certainly have reason to if you're the monster you're imagining."

The truth of her words surprised her. Even with her history, she wasn't running. She seemed to know, better than Brendan did himself, that he could never hurt anyone.

"I could be."

"No, you couldn't." Despair gripped her. How could she reach him? "You're willing to offer second chances to every person you meet. How is it you can't give the same opportunity to yourself? Why can't you turn this over to that God you claim cares about everyone?"

"I've tried. Don't you know I'd try?" It was a cry from his heart. "I've asked Him over and over to take my temper away. He doesn't answer."

He took a long, shaky breath and shook his head, as if that final revelation made him aware of how much he'd told her. He took a careful step away from her, and her hand dropped from his arm.

"Brendan—"

"Don't." He held up his hand, stopping anything she might try to say. "I can't talk about this anymore, Claire. Please, just forget what I said. This is my battle to deal with, not yours."

Not yours. He might as well have said he didn't want or need her, because that was what he meant.

She took a step back, recognizing the insurmountable barrier between them for what it was. It wasn't her background or his family history that stood between them, or his faith and her lack of it.

It was Brendan himself. He believed in that darkness inside him. She had no power that could counter that.

Half an hour later, Claire had managed to wash away all traces of tears from her face. Okay. She reached for the door into the sanctuary. She'd better see what kind of a mess she still had to deal with.

She had to concentrate on that, because if she let herself think about Brendan, she just might fall apart entirely.

She opened the door and stepped inside. Her breath caught. Everything looked the way it should.

Stacy and Amy were adjusting the final ribbons on the pews. Several of the boys wielded brooms and dustpans with more energy than skill.

"Wow." She glanced from one concerned young face to another. "You've put it all back. How on earth did you manage?"

"Rick called me, so Amy and I came right over." Stacy sent a scathing glance toward the boys. "I knew we couldn't count on them to fix things the way they should be."

"Well, you did a wonderful job. All of you." To her

embarrassment, tears stung her eyes. She absolutely couldn't let herself start crying again. "I'm so grateful."

"It does look pretty good." Stacy's proprietary tone made Claire smile. "Okay, guys, you can put those things back where you got them. Make sure everything's put away."

The boys, apparently thoroughly cowed, hurried out.

Claire, watching them, noticed that someone was missing. "What happened to Rick? Did he run out on you?"

Stacy gathered up the last fragments of ribbon. "No, he had something to do. He went to see that Mr. Gray. He's going to make things right for the Rev."

Rick Romero, bearding Harvey Gray in his den. Rick would probably never get in to see him, but she could only shudder to think of Gray's reaction if he did. Not that there was anything at all that she could do about it.

"We're gonna get out of here." Stacy paused by the door. "Are you okay?"

She nodded, sinking down on the closest pew. "I'm fine. You go ahead. I'll turn off the lights and take a last look around before I go. And Stacy? Thanks."

Stacy gave her a confident grin and followed Amy out of the sanctuary.

When had Stacy gained so much confidence in her own abilities?

She and Stacy seemed to have switched places. She'd lost confidence that she could do anything about anything.

It was true. She leaned back against the pew, too tired to move. She couldn't do anything about the situation between Rick and Gray. And she couldn't do anything about the pain Brendan was suffering.

She tilted her head back, looking up at the stained-glass window above her, lit from outside by the slanting rays of the setting sun. Jesus walking on the water, reaching out toward Peter, sinking in the waves.

It was funny that the stories from her childhood came so readily to mind, as if they'd been waiting all these years for her to need them again. She remembered how that story went.

Peter had climbed out of the boat, trying to walk toward Jesus on the water. But when he'd stopped trusting, he'd begun to sink.

She was sinking, too—sinking under the weight of all the things she wanted to control and couldn't. She blinked as tears filled her eyes. How had she gotten to this place? She'd built her life around controlling every aspect of her world.

She didn't really need to ask the question. She knew how she'd come here. Brendan.

Her heart twisted. Brendan.

*He's Your servant, isn't he? Why aren't You helping him when he needs You most?*

The tears slid down her face, appalling her. She never cried. She never lost control of her life.

She tried to wipe the tears away, but they wouldn't stop flowing. Her throat caught in a painful sob. The tears poured down, as if washing away a lifetime of regret, pain and mistakes.

She looked up at the stained-glass face, which shimmered through her tears.

*I believed in You once, a long time ago. Why did I stop? Do You care?*

The silence in the sanctuary seemed to shiver, as if the very walls would speak to her. And then she felt the wordless Voice in her heart. She knew she'd heard the same Voice in her heart, a long time ago.

*Come unto Me, all ye who labor and are heavy-laden, and I will give you rest.*

It had been her mother's favorite verse, repeated over and over during the last months of her life.

She didn't have to worry about being strong any longer. The tears spilled down, and she didn't bother to wipe them away. She could be weak. She could depend upon His strength, not her own.

## *Chapter Fifteen*

Brendan stood at the top of the chancel steps, watching as Claire came down the center aisle. The dress Nolie had chosen for her maid of honor was jade green, and against it Claire's skin looked like cream. If a faint unhappiness shadowed her eyes, probably no one noticed but him.

She was beautiful, inside and out, he saw that now. But she wasn't for him.

Any remaining doubts in his mind had been erased by what happened the previous day with the teens. The darkness he feared did lurk inside him, and if he weren't constantly on guard, it would engulf him.

That was bad enough for him as a man and as a minister. It would be far worse if he married. He'd already known he couldn't take that risk. He hadn't even realized that deep inside he'd been thinking of Claire in that way. Dreaming that somehow they might have a life together.

Now he knew that was impossible.

Nothing is impossible with God.

The echo in his mind seemed to mock him. Of course, nothing was impossible for God, but he'd begged again and again for God to take the anger away, and the answer had been no.

Claire's slow progress down the aisle came to a halt as she turned to face Gabe and Seth, Gabe's best man. Now she was in profile to him. He couldn't continue staring at her. People would notice.

He forced his gaze across the congregation. It looked as if nearly everyone who'd been invited had come. Nolie didn't have any family, but the Flanagan clan more than made up for that lack with friends, relatives and firefighters who cheerfully overflowed to the bride's side of the church.

Ryan, his ushering duties completed, slipped into the front pew with his mother, sisters and assorted children. Nolie had said that if they were going to have this wedding, it would be the wedding they wanted, not the one the etiquette books said they should have. So there were only two attendants instead of four or five, and the ushering crew came from Gabe's old squad at the fire-house and wore uniforms instead of tuxes. The bride was being escorted down the aisle by her new father-in-law, which suited her just fine.

The organ music swelled and changed. Every person in the church turned to look back the center aisle.

Joe Flanagan stepped carefully into the aisle, and a

murmur of appreciation swept across the sanctuary at the sight of the woman on his arm. Nolie was radiant, her pale gold hair swept up and then cascading down over the ivory lace of her gown. But it wasn't her appearance that caused that wave of happiness at the sight of her.

It was the triumphant love that shimmered like a golden bond from Nolie to Gabe and back again, seeming to encompass every person within reach. No one who saw them could doubt that they were destined by God to be together. No one could watch Nolie move down the aisle toward her waiting groom and fail to be touched by the sight.

Mary Kate was clasping Kenny's hand, and Terry wiped her eyes with a lacy handkerchief, which she then passed to Stacy, equally tearful, beside her. In spite of his own unhappiness, Brendan was swept with joy.

Nolie and Gabe's wedding wasn't just for the two of them. It was a reaffirmation of God's love, acted out through them for every person here.

Nolie came to a halt in front of him. Joe, looking as proud as if she were really one of his children, put her hand in Gabe's and then bent to kiss her cheek. As he moved back to join Siobhan in the pew, Claire arranged Nolie's train, her movements swift and graceful. He could see the tears that shimmered in her eyes.

He hoped they were tears of pride and happiness. She deserved to feel proud of all she'd accomplished in putting this wedding together. No one could have worked harder or cared more.

And she'd done it while dealing with a host of emotionally wrenching events in her own life. Because of him. If it had not been for his blundering intrusion into her life, she'd have been spared a lot of pain.

So would he.

He opened the worship book and smiled at Gabe and Nolie across it. This was not going to be easy.

"Dearly beloved, we are gathered here in the sight of God and these witnesses…"

The words carried him along. This was right, and he could take joy in that in spite of his own pain.

His glance intersected with Claire's. He read the truth there. Claire was thinking the same thing he was. That this could have been them. Could still be, if he could conquer his weakness.

*Please, Lord.*

His voice was steady as he went on with the service. Only God could hear the anguished cry of his soul.

*Help me. Please. Help me.*

Claire didn't know how she'd gotten through the ceremony. To stand so close to Brendan, to see Nolie and Gabe's happiness, to know she and Brendan would never have that—

Well, she'd managed. She moved through the crowd of people in Fellowship Hall. The happy buzz of conversation and snippets she heard here and there told her everyone was surprised and pleased at the transformation she and Stacy had managed to achieve in the utilitarian room.

Her gaze automatically assessed the caterer's people and the teens who'd volunteered to work at the reception. They were circulating with trays of hot and cold appetizers, just as they should be.

She'd survived the service, and no one would know that the smile she wore felt stiff and artificial on her lips. She'd thought her feelings would ease once the reception started. After all, Brendan was clear across the room, with close to a hundred people between them.

That didn't seem to matter. Apparently she didn't have to be near Brendan to feel his presence. She was aware of his every expression and movement no matter where he was, as if they were connected at an unseen level.

*This is so painful. Why did You bring me close to You, only to lose Brendan?*

There didn't seem to be an answer to that, but she still felt the loving warmth of God's presence. He wouldn't let her down the way her earthly father had.

"Everything looks wonderful." Siobhan paused to give her a quick hug. Siobhan's silver lace dress brought out her slender elegance, but it was the happiness on her face that people would remember.

"Thanks to lots of help from you." She'd never been much for hugging, but it felt good to have Siobhan's arm around her. "Do you think the appetizers are making it all the way through the crowd?"

"I think you should relax and enjoy this," Siobhan said. "You've earned it, and everyone is having a wonderful time." She laughed. "People can't believe this old hall can look so good."

"Amazing what you can do with some fabric netting and a few dozen strings of lights, isn't it?" She looked around. "You know, I think I'm taking more pride in this than in any professional accomplishment."

"Of course." Siobhan's voice was warm. "You did this for love. That makes all the difference."

*Love.* The word set up a bittersweet echo in her heart.

She loved Brendan. She thought he loved her, but she knew he'd never admit to his feelings as long as he held on to the fear that he'd inherited his father's rage.

Her throat closed. She squeezed Siobhan's hand. "I'm going to check on things in the kitchen. I'll catch up with you later."

She moved through the crowd, her radar informing her that Brendan was talking with some of his cousins. His face had relaxed, and a peal of laughter rang out from the group.

For an instant she felt a pang of envy. The Flanagan family never needed to question the bond they had with each other.

The kitchen door swung sharply open as she approached. Amy, a tray of shrimp puffs balanced on one hand, hurried through. In a simple black skirt and white shirt and her hair pulled back, the girl looked totally different.

"Amy, you look so pretty. Is everything going all right?"

The girl's smile would have lit the room. "Great. The caterer told me I was the best helper he'd had in a long time, and if I ever wanted a job, I should come to him."

"That is great." It had taken so little to give the girl a sense of accomplishment. "Have you seen Stacy? I haven't talked to her since before the ceremony."

"Not in a while." Amy proffered the tray. "Want to try one? I should get these out while they're still hot."

Claire slid one of the steaming puffs onto a napkin and then watched as Amy worked her way through the crowd, as smiling and gracious as if she were the hostess. If the other kids were working out as well as Amy, that would be amazing.

Her gaze swept the room, identifying her workers. Everyone seemed to be concentrating on the task at hand. Odd, that she still didn't see Stacy anywhere. She'd have expected her to be reveling in this experience. The girl had been so excited about the wedding.

A tiny figure hurtled out of the crowd, and Claire stooped to catch Seth's little boy before he could crash into the kitchen door.

"Thanks, Claire." Terry, following the child, sounded breathless. "I'm supposed to be watching Davy while Seth attends to his best man duties. Are all two-year-olds this fast?" She scooped up the toddler, kissing him until he squealed.

Terry moved off with the child, who giggled and twisted in her arms. Little Davy didn't have a mother, but the rest of the Flanagans managed to shower him with love to spare.

"Claire."

Her worry jagged upward as she turned to find Harvey Gray standing next to her.

"Mr. Gray. Are you enjoying the celebration?"

He nodded, seemed to realize he had a cracker piled with pâté in his hand, and popped it into his mouth. "Very nice." He swallowed. "Are you responsible for these teenagers who are working for the caterer?"

She could feel her anxiety start to increase and then suddenly deflated as if punctured. She didn't have to react that way to Gray's every whim any longer. Her future was in God's hands, not her employer's.

"Yes, I've been helping the pastor with them." She wasn't going to hide her involvement. "I thought this might be good work experience."

Gray frowned, but before he could respond, Brendan strode up to join them. Her heart gave that familiar little jolt at his presence.

"How is everything going?" The wariness in Brendan's eyes told a story. He'd joined them because he feared Gray was blaming her for the kids' involvement. He wanted to protect her.

She smiled, feeling ridiculously warmed at the evidence of his caring. "So far, so good. I won't really relax until the last slice of cake has been served, though."

Gray sent a lowering glance from her to Brendan. "I

suppose you know that one of your teens came to see me yesterday."

Brendan's tension was evident in the tightening of his jaw and the fine lines that formed around his mouth. "One of my kids? No, I didn't know that. Which one?"

"Rick Romero."

She could almost feel Brendan wince. "Why did he come to see you?"

To make things right for the Rev. How much worse had Rick made things by his well-meant act?

"He wanted to talk to me about you." Gray frowned. Brendan's eyes found hers. "Did you know about this?"

"The other kids told me he'd gone."

"Why didn't you tell—" He stopped. If he thought about it, he'd know why she hadn't come back to tell him.

Gray cleared his throat. "I'm not sure why I agreed to see him, but I was impressed."

"Impressed?" Brendan sounded as shocked as she felt.

"Kid was smarter than I'd expected." Gray had the tone of someone determined to be fair. "He made some sense, actually. Explained what you were trying to do with those kids."

"Rick made sense." Brendan sounded as if he had trouble accepting that.

Gray nodded. "Thing is, Pastor, you're going about it all wrong."

"I am?"

"If you want to make those street kids employable,

you've got to involve some of the business people. We're the ones who know what it takes. You shouldn't be trying to do it by yourself."

Gray could not have had a bigger effect if he'd used a two-by-four. "You mean you'd be willing to help?"

He put his hand on Brendan's shoulder. "I have some ideas for how we can go about it. We need to get a few other businessmen on board. And women, too, to give the girls some good role models. Claire can help us there."

"Of course I will."

Claire took a step back, letting the conversation flow between them. It was going to be all right. In another half hour, Harvey Gray would be convinced that the whole project had been his idea to begin with.

Brendan caught her eye over Gray's shoulder, and she found she could smile at him without pain. This was going to be all right. Brendan's job and his ministry were safe.

As for her—she looked at the sudden change in her feelings in astonishment. She was going to be all right, too. Even if she couldn't have the love she wanted, she had friends, people who were as close as family. She had satisfying work to do and people she could help.

God had a good life ahead for her, even if that life didn't include Brendan.

Tears stung her eyes, but her heart felt whole. "Thank You," she whispered. *Thank You.*

Brendan wove his way through the chattering crowd, intent on finding Claire again. She'd slipped away from his conversation with her boss, and he had to tell her what had happened.

His steps slowed. That strong need to share things—good and bad—with Claire hit him out of the blue. He shouldn't burden Claire with those confidences when he couldn't offer her anything more, but she had to know about this.

He spotted her then. She stood near the kitchen door, seeming to scan the room. He worked his way toward her.

"Hi. Looking for someone?"

She nodded. "It's odd that Stacy's not around. Have you seen her since the ceremony?"

"The last time I saw her, she was mopping up tears. Maybe she went to freshen up."

"I'll check the ladies' room."

"Can you give me a minute first?"

She nodded, eyes questioning.

He touched her hand to draw her out of the crowd and then quickly took his hand away. He shouldn't give in to that need to touch her.

"Could you believe that turnaround Harvey Gray did?" He lowered his voice, although it was unlikely anyone could hear him in the din. "By the time we finished talking, he was acting as if the drop-in project was all his idea."

She smiled. "If I were you, I'd just let him go on thinking that. Once he's bought into something to that extent, he won't let you down."

"Rick must have been more persuasive than I've ever

given him credit for. Or Harvey's more civic-minded."
He found that thought sobering. Hadn't he believed that
other people could see the right thing and do it?

"Maybe you need to give them a chance to minister,
too. You don't have to do everything yourself, you know."

He could only stare at her. "How did you get so smart
about ministry?"

Was this the woman who'd openly proclaimed she
didn't need the church in her life? Claire seemed to
have depths he hadn't expected, too.

"You pushed me into helping with Stacy, remember?" Her smile was softer than he'd ever seen it. "I
gained as much as she did from that experience. Is it so
hard to believe that a man like Harvey Gray might ben-
efit from doing something for someone else?"

"You make it sound like I've been acting spiritually
superior to everyone else." He hadn't, had he? He found
he didn't like the image that created.

"No, not in that sense. But you do seem to think you
have to do everything yourself. I guess I recognize that
because I'm that way, too."

"Kindred spirits," he said, and then wished he hadn't.
He wanted—

Well, maybe it was safer not to think too much about
what he wanted.

"Yes." Her smile wavered for an instant. "Your aunt
says you've always had too great a sense of responsibility. Maybe it's time you shared some of that responsibility with your parishioners."

"Aunt Siobhan knows me better than anyone." Except you, Claire. "Maybe I'd better start taking her good advice. And yours."

"So you're going to find yourself working with Harvey Gray, and giving him credit for the program."

She seemed intent on keeping herself out of the equation. He couldn't blame her for that.

"He can have all the credit he wants, as long as the kids are being helped."

"To say nothing of your job being safe."

"That, too." He smiled. "I have a feeling you're responsible for this, no matter how much you deny it. After all, if you hadn't taught Rick whatever he knows about relating to people like Gray, he'd never have succeeded."

"He's—"

A ringing stopped her words, and she fumbled in the green silk bag that matched her dress.

"You're not telling me you brought a cell phone to the wedding, are you?"

She fished the phone out. "It was turned off during the ceremony, Pastor." She put it to her ear.

The smile faded from her lips, and her face paled. He grasped her hand.

"What is it? What's wrong?"

Her eyes met his, and the fear he saw there cut him to the bone.

"It's Stacy." Her voice was barely more than a whisper. "She's not here. She's at Ted's. She's in danger."

# Chapter Sixteen

For just a moment, Claire's mind seemed to freeze completely. She couldn't move. She couldn't form any image except that of falling—falling, helpless to protect—

No. She shook off the thought, realizing that Brendan was gripping her hands fiercely in his.

"What did she say?"

She forced herself to concentrate. "She said something about having to talk to Ted, but he's refusing to let her leave."

"It's going to be okay," he said. "We'll go right now. We'll take care of her."

Now her mind spun recklessly from one obligation to another. This was the day she'd planned for weeks. How could she walk away?

"The reception—they haven't even served the meal yet. What am I going to do?"

His hands held hers. "You're not going to try to do it all yourself, remember?"

She took a breath, her gaze meeting his. The concern she saw there warmed her, and she knew he was right. It was time to let go of her obsessive need to control everything. "I don't have to. Do you see Siobhan or Mary Kate?"

He nodded, raising his hand, and in a moment Siobhan slipped through the crowd to them.

"Something's wrong. What is it?" Her blue eyes went dark with concern.

"Stacy's in trouble. We've got to go," Brendan said rapidly. "We need you to take over here."

Claire managed another breath, trying to organize the things Siobhan needed to know. Don't panic. It will be all right.

"The caterer is probably about ready to start serving. Maybe you can deal with him and have Seth take responsibility for getting everyone seated." She pressed her hands to her temples, hoping she wasn't letting anything drop. "If we're not back by the time you're ready to serve the cake—"

"Don't even think about it." Siobhan's arms went around her in a quick, reassuring hug. "You just go to Stacy. She's the one who needs you now. We'll take care of everything here, I promise."

Siobhan was right. She didn't have to issue orders or send memos or stand over them to make sure everything was done the way she wanted. They would take care of everything.

"Thank you." She pressed her cheek against Siobhan's. "We'll call you as soon as we can."

"We'll be praying."

Brendan caught her hand and led her toward the kitchen door. "We'd better go out the back. My car is there, and it will be easier to get away without too many people noticing."

They hurried through the kitchen. From the corner of her eye she spotted the caterer gaping at her. She felt a flicker of panic. She should explain—

But then she saw Siobhan taking his arm and knew she didn't have to. Siobhan would handle it.

They ran to the car. In an instant, it seemed, Brendan had spun out of the lot.

"It's not far." He took the corner quickly. "We'll get there in time. And Ted probably knows she called us. He won't do anything stupid."

She could only manage to nod, her hands clasping each other tightly.

*Please, Father. Be with Stacy. She needs Your help. Protect her.*

The words echoed in her mind. And then she realized who else needed her prayers.

*Ted.* Her heart rebelled, but she forced the words to form. *Be with him, too, Father. I don't really want to pray for him, but I know he needs help. He's just as lost as she is.*

The truth of her own prayer hit her then. Ted was lost. No matter how much anger she felt at him for what he'd done, she had to feel sorrow, too.

"Claire? Are you all right?" Brendan gave her a concerned glance.

"I'm okay." Then she realized he meant her silence. "I was praying."

It seemed to take him a moment to digest that. "You were praying."

"Yes." She stared out the window for a moment, blanking out the view of busy streets. There was no reason to keep this from Brendan, and every reason to tell him.

"I've found my way back." The words cost her an effort, but she managed them. "I didn't want to. I didn't even realize I was lost." She looked at him. "There's something else to your credit, Pastor. Thanks to you, I began to realize what was missing in my life."

Brendan reached across to grip her hand, and she saw that his eyes were bright with unshed tears. "I'm glad, Claire. Very glad."

She smiled. "I thought you might be."

He squeezed her fingers and then grabbed the wheel again to take the turn onto Second Street.

"I don't think I deserve any credit, though." He shook his head. "I haven't been a very sterling example of what a Christian should be."

"Yes. You have," she said softly. More than you know, I'm afraid.

A wave of sorrow swept over her. Her lack of faith—

the thing that could have been the biggest barrier between them—had disappeared, but that didn't matter. Brendan was as far away as ever.

She suppressed the thought. All her concern now had to be for Stacy. There'd be plenty of time ahead to get past what might have been between her and Brendan. She was going to be fine, but Stacy—

"Why on earth did she go there?" The question burst out of her. "She must have slipped out as soon as the ceremony was over. What could she have been thinking?"

"I wish I knew." Brendan leaned forward, scanning the crowded block for a parking space. "I thought she trusted us enough now to tell someone what she was doing."

"She knew we wouldn't let her go alone." She grasped the armrest as Brendan jolted the car up onto the curb. "What are you doing?"

He was already on the sidewalk, and she slid out of the car to follow him.

"I'll worry about a ticket later." He yanked the building door open, releasing the stale smell of the dusty stairwell. Then he stopped, looking at her. "Stay here. Please, Claire. You shouldn't go in."

For an instant, as she stared at the steep wooden stairs, the fear took over. Falling—

"No." She swallowed hard, choking down the fear. "I'm still afraid, but it's not going to paralyze me. I can let God handle it for me."

She pushed past him, starting up the stairs, and she heard the thud of his footsteps behind her.

*Please, Lord. Please, Lord.*

The words of the prayer seemed to keep time with their rush up the stairs. They weren't alone. He was with them.

And Siobhan and the others who were praying for them right now. They weren't alone.

She would never be alone again.

Claire had found a way to deal with her fears, Brendan realized. He grabbed the rail to propel himself up the last few steps. She was still afraid, but now she trusted God to carry her through.

In spite of his fears for Stacy and for Ted, a fierce happiness swept through him. *Thank You, Father. Thank You for bringing Claire back to You.*

They reached the hallway. He didn't bother to knock. He just grabbed the door and shoved, and it flew open. The force of his forward movement carried him clear into the room. Claire was right behind him.

Stacy cowered against the refrigerator, the table cluttered with pizza boxes and hamburger wrappers between her and Ted. Ted swung around at their entrance, his big hands doubling into fists, but Brendan's first thought was for Stacy.

"Stacy. Are you all right?"

The girl nodded, choking on a sob. Her face was tear-stained but otherwise unmarked, and the turquoise silk dress Claire had bought her for the wedding didn't show signs of a struggle.

*Thank You, Father. You brought us here in time.*

"What are you doing here? We don't want you." Ted swayed a little. The boy had been obviously been drinking.

An acrid taste formed in his mouth. Drinking and anger made a dangerous combination. He certainly knew that as well as anyone. His father—

No. He wouldn't let that thought in.

"Maybe you don't, Ted." He moved slowly toward the boy, keeping his voice low. "But Stacy does. She called and asked us to come and talk with you."

"She doesn't want you. She doesn't need anybody but me. She knows I'll take care of her."

"Ted, look at me." If he could keep the kid focused on him it would give Claire a chance to get to Stacy. "You know I wouldn't lie to you, don't you?"

Ted lowered his head, shaking it as if trying to think through the fog of alcohol. "No. I guess you always been square with me, Rev."

The familiar nickname eased the tension inside him by a hair. If Ted was still reachable by reason, they had a chance to get through this situation without any further grief.

"I'm telling you the truth now. You can't resolve things with Stacy by scaring her or telling her what to do."

"I'm not."

Brendan sensed, rather than saw, Claire moving toward Stacy. The girl seemed frozen to the spot. If they were going to get her out of here, they'd have to take her.

Claire was afraid. But she was doing it anyway.

"Yes, I think you are." He took another step, bringing him almost within arm's reach of the boy. "She wouldn't have called us unless you'd scared her."

"She shouldn't have done that. I told her. All I want to do is make things right with her."

"How are you going to do that?" His voice sharpened as the boy's head moved, as if he'd look toward Stacy. "Look at me. How will you make things right?"

"I said I'd marry her." The kid's face screwed up, and he looked like a six-year-old about to cry.

But Ted wasn't a six-year-old. He was a confused, angry seventeen-year-old with a grown man's strength and a dangerous temper.

"Isn't that the right thing to do?" Ted's voice shot up. He thrust his face toward Brendan belligerently. "Isn't it? If you'd leave us alone, we'd take care of ourselves."

Brendan felt his own anger, black and ugly, boil under the surface. He'd lost control when Rick had done something minor in comparison to this. What might he do if Ted went after the women?

"Come on, Ted. You don't believe that."

It took more strength than he'd known he had to keep his voice even. Claire had reached Stacy now, knowing what he wanted her to do without the need for words. She started edging Stacy, a step at a time, toward the door.

They were going to make it. If Claire could just get Stacy outside without anything going wrong, they'd be okay. Ted wouldn't start swinging. He wouldn't lose control.

"Stacy loves me. Tell them, Stacy."

Just that quickly, the situation disintegrated out of control. Ted swung toward Stacy as he said the words and saw what Claire was doing. With a muttered curse, he launched himself toward Claire and Stacy.

Brendan flew across the few feet of space and got between them. Ted barreled into him, and he grabbed the boy, feeling his anger surge, hot and reckless, ready to strike out.

"Claire, get out of here. Now."

He heard the door, the rush of their footsteps, the door slamming closed. Then Ted's fist connected with his jaw and for an instant he didn't hear anything.

He struggled with the boy, trying to hold on to him, trying to control himself, fearing that if he struck back he wouldn't be able to stop, he'd be like his father—

No. He couldn't control the anger. He saw the truth of that.

But God could. Relief flooded through him. God could.

He clamped his arms tightly around Ted, absorbing the kid's struggles with his own body as he realized the truth. He didn't have to do it himself. All he had to do was give God the control.

The fight seemed to go out of Ted. He stumbled back a step, his eyes searching Brendan's face.

"I was just trying to do the right thing. Isn't getting married the right thing?"

He seemed to see his parents more clearly than he ever had before. They'd married, but they'd brought out the worst in each other, turning their home into a battlefield.

"Not always." He put his hand on the boy's shoulder. "The right thing has to be what's best for Stacy and the baby. That might mean giving up both of them before someone gets hurt."

Ted's face crumpled, tears spurting from his eyes. "I don't want to hurt anyone. I don't. But I can't stop. You gotta help me."

"I know." *Thank You, Father.* "I will."

The reception was drawing to a close. Claire stood near the cake table, watching as Gabe and Nolie said goodbye to their guests. She'd missed most of the reception, but she didn't have any regrets.

"Did you get a piece of cake?"

She discovered she could look at Brendan without wincing. That was a step forward, wasn't it?

"A little one. How about you?"

He nodded. "I shared it with Stacy. She seems to be recovering." He paused a moment. "I didn't want to ask her any questions, but did she ever tell you what made her go to Ted's?"

"She said it was because of the wedding." She blinked back the tears that wanted to spill over whenever she thought of the girl's words. "She said that being involved with the wedding made her see what marriage is supposed to be. She realized that neither she nor Ted is ready for that, so she went there to tell him so."

Tears seemed to sparkle in Brendan's eyes, too. "Well." He cleared his throat. "Maybe the future is looking up for Stacy and her baby. And for Ted."

"Bittersweet." Amazing how appropriate that word was for her feelings as well as Stacy's. "She's going to give the baby up for adoption. It'll break her heart, but she knows it's the right thing to do."

"She's going to need a lot of support."

She smiled, brushing away the tears. "She's going to get it." Stacy would have the support she hadn't had, and that would make all the difference.

"Yes. She is." Their eyes connected, and he seemed to know exactly what she was thinking. He smiled. "You should be happy, Claire. You did exactly what you said you were going to do. You put on the perfect wedding for Gabe and Nolie."

"It didn't turn out quite the way I intended."

"Weddings never do."

"I guess not." She watched as Gabe swung Nolie into his arms for a kiss. "They're happy, that's the important thing." She shrugged. "So I am, too."

She was. That was the most amazing thing. She might not have the happily-ever-after that Nolie did, but she'd rediscovered her faith and with it came a whole new world of useful things to do.

Her life wouldn't be focused solely on work and ambition any longer. She'd be happy, even if Brendan wouldn't be a part of her future.

"All of this—" She gestured at the room, which was

emptying now but seemed to still hold on to the happiness that had filled it. "Putting on this wedding has changed me. For the better, I hope."

He smiled. "Me, too."

"You mean now you appreciate all the work that goes into putting on a wedding?"

"I'll never be impatient with a wedding planner again, I promise you." His eyes grew serious. "But that's not all." He shook his head. "I thought I could go on the way I was. I thought I could suppress the memories of my parents along with my anger. I thought I could live for my work."

Something about his intent look had set up a fluttering inside her, as if her whole being trembled in response. "You don't feel that any longer?"

"Not since you." He captured her hands, holding them in a warm clasp. "Knowing you, caring about you—I had to face what I was doing. Once I had, I knew I couldn't live that way any longer."

He was echoing what she'd been thinking. Once she'd known him, she couldn't live in her nice safe world of work any longer. She'd had to have more.

"Knowing you forced me to confront the darkness inside me." For an instant his eyes looked so bleak that her heart wept for him. Then he shook his head. "You were right. I hadn't trusted God with it. I just kept asking Him to take my anger away, instead of realizing that I could depend on Him to control it."

Her fingers closed on his. "I knew that all along, you know. I knew it wasn't possible for you to hurt anyone."

"Then you knew me better than I knew myself."

His voice had deepened with emotion, and her tears threatened to spill over again. God had healed the wounds the past had inflicted on them. She really couldn't ask for anything else.

"I was just thinking—" he lifted their clasped hands to his lips and pressed a kiss against her fingers "—do you suppose that our wedding could be a little less perfect than Nolie and Gabe's?"

She could only stare at him, seeing the flame in his eyes as he held her hand against his cheek.

"I love you, Claire. Now, and forever. Maybe we're not there yet, maybe you need more time. But I don't. I know I want a life with you, if you're willing to take a chance on a man with a past like mine."

The love that pulsed through her seemed to sweep everything else from its path. "There's nothing chancy about it, Pastor. You must know that." She cradled his cheek with her palm. "I love you. Forever."

It was a promise, as solemn and joyous as the ones they'd take in front of God one day. For both of them, the past was just a prologue to the life God planned for them together.

\* \* \* \* \*

Dear Reader,

I'm so glad you decided to pick up this book and I hope
my story touched your heart. The faith struggle Claire
and Brendan went through on their way to a happy
ending meant a lot to me.

I found it fun to relive the excitement and stress of
planning a wedding. I don't think there's anyone who
doesn't have a story to tell of all the things that went
wrong!

I hope you'll write and let me know how you liked this
story. Address your letter to me at Steeple Hill Books,
233 Broadway, Suite 1001, New York, NY 10279,
and I'll be happy to send you a signed bookplate
or bookmark. You can also visit me on the Web at
www.martaperry.com, or e-mail me at
marta@martaperry.com.

Blessings,

Marta Perry

# Love Inspired

## LOVING PROMISES

### BY

## GAIL GAYMER MARTIN

Cynical businessman Dale Levin had a unique attitude toward marriage—it could never come close to what his parents shared, and caring for them showed him that even true love could end. He vowed never to marry, but when he met widowed Bev Miller and her boisterous children, he wondered if God was granting him the happy ending he secretly craved....

## Don't miss LOVING PROMISES
### On sale March 2005

*Available at your favorite retail outlet*

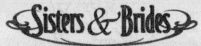

# Take 2 inspirational love stories FREE!

## PLUS get a FREE surprise gift!

### Mail to Steeple Hill Reader Service™

**In U.S.**
3010 Walden Ave.
P.O. Box 1867
Buffalo, NY 14240-1867

**In Canada**
P.O. Box 609
Fort Erie, Ontario
L2A 5X3

**YES!** Please send me 2 free Love Inspired® novels and my free surprise gift. After receiving them, if I don't wish to receive anymore, I can return the shipping statement marked cancel. If I don't cancel, I will receive 4 brand-new novels every month, before they're available in stores! Bill me at the low price of $4.24 each in the U.S. and $4.74 each in Canada, plus 25¢ shipping and handling and applicable sales tax, if any*. That's the complete price and a savings of over 10% off the cover prices—quite a bargain! I understand that accepting the books and gift places me under no obligation ever to buy any books. I can always return a shipment and cancel at any time. Even if I never buy another book from Steeple Hill, the 2 free books and the surprise gift are mine to keep forever.

113 IDN DZ9M
313 IDN DZ9N

| Name | (PLEASE PRINT) | |
| --- | --- | --- |
| Address | Apt. No. | |
| City | State/Prov. | Zip/Postal Code |

**Not valid to current Love Inspired® subscribers.**

*Want to try two free books from another series?*
**Call 1-800-873-8635 or visit www.morefreebooks.com.**

\* Terms and prices are subject to change without notice. Sales tax applicable in New York. Canadian residents will be charged applicable provincial taxes and GST. All orders subject to approval. Offer limited to one per household.

® are registered trademarks owned and used by the trademark owner and or its licensee.

INTLI04R                    ©2004 Steeple Hill

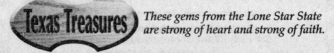